An American Tapestry

Patricia Hamilton Slagle

An American Tapestry

ISBN: 979-8-218-81472-4

Prologue

The paper, once sturdy and sharp with ink, had softened with age, its edges curling as time wore on. Yet the words it bore still clung to the page, as though refusing to let go. These tomes, fragile as they were, had been slipped into books, secured in scrapbooks on yellowed pages, and secreted in diaries tied with now-frayed ribbons, containing letters of happy and sorrowful times, love, and tenderness, safeguarded through the years.

The Loomis and Parsons families, bound by more than blood, had preserved their past through ink and memory, each generation passing down not just a name but a responsibility—*to remember*. It was more than sentimentality. It was an effort to hold back time's relentless erosion, a way to ensure that the past, despite the world's ceaseless forward march, would remain.

And it did.

Now, as I sit with these papers in my hands—once only spoken of in my mother's stories—I am grateful. Grateful not just for the stories but for the realization that I have inherited more than I imagined. What was once distant—the world of my great-great-grandparents and their children—has become immediate and personal. Through their words, I've come to understand them not as names in a family tree but as real people—flesh and blood, with hopes, struggles, and lives that resonate deeply with my own.

Contents

Part 1
The Loomis Family

"Few families can rival the records of the distinguished Loomis family in its achievements over some ten generations of its residence in this country."

"Ne cede malis"

(Do not give way to misfortunes.)

— Lomas, Lomax, Loomis Family Motto

1

Windsor, Connecticut Beckons

The year was 1638.

The Three Kingdoms—England, Scotland, and Ireland—teetered under the rule of Charles I, their people divided between loyalty to the Crown and a rising murmur of discontent in streets and town squares.

King Charles I clung tightly to the doctrine of the Divine Right of Kings—a belief that monarchs ruled by the will of God alone—at a time when such convictions were rapidly falling out of favor.

Parliament, once a pliant advisory body, had begun to find its voice. Its members no longer saw themselves as mere ornaments to royal authority, but as stewards of the realm, demanding control over taxation, legislation, and the direction of national policy.

This growing tension took on the shape of a quiet revolution. Parliament sought not to depose the king but to bind him—to establish, in law, that even a monarch could be held accountable.

Charles's repeated levying of taxes without parliamentary consent, often to fund his costly and unpopular military ventures, was viewed not just as overreach but as a betrayal. And when he dissolved Parliament—once, twice, then *again and again*—it was seen not as the act of a sovereign protecting his crown, but as a tyrant flouting the very rights of his people.

For many, these power struggles were no longer abstract disputes between lords and kings—they reached into hearths and homes. The kingdom's unrest began to fray daily life. To stay was to endure the uncertainty of a country unraveling. To leave was to gamble everything on an unknown land across the sea.

Joseph Loomis had not been the first to consider the journey, nor would he be the last.

Born in the market town of Braintree in Essex, England, he had built a life many would envy. A woolen draper by trade—a respected profession that blended textile knowledge with the precision of a tailor—Joseph had, by his late forties, achieved what most in his station only hoped for.

He held a standing in the community, owned property—his father had named him the primary heir to the family estate, a rare position of honor in a time when primogeniture often determined such matters—and served in the local constabulary. His household was full; his children, many of them nearly grown, would have been preparing to take up trades or marry into other reputable families.

By all accounts, he was settled. And yet, he left.

To a man like Joseph Loomis, prudent and forward-looking, the question may not have been why leave, but why stay. In America, land could be owned outright and passed freely to one's children. There were no guild restrictions, no royal monopolies, and fewer layers of patronage. One could build not only a life, but a lineage. *So, he took the gamble.*

As the ship *'Susan and Ellen'* swayed beneath them, creaking with the burden of families who had wagered their futures on this voyage, he knew there was no turning back.

This was to be their new *home.*

Though already well established in England, he was not a man to confuse comfort with permanence. They spent a year in Dorchester—long enough to find their footing but not long enough to grow roots.

Inland, along the broad Connecticut River, something new was taking shape. The settlements of Windsor, Hartford, and Wethersfield had recently united under a written constitution— an unheard-of document that offered settlers not only land but a say in their governance. It promised stability born not of royal decree, but of community will.

To a man like Joseph, who prized self-determination, that must have meant everything.

By February 1640, Joseph Loomis secured 21 acres of land at the meeting point of the Farmington and Connecticut Rivers—a prime location, both agriculturally rich and strategically situated near essential water routes that connected the growing settlements of the Connecticut Valley. These rivers were vital thoroughfares for transporting goods, news, and livestock, and the land surrounding them—cleared gradually through community effort and individual labor—formed the backbone of Windsor's early economy.

The family made a life there, not all at once, but in patient increments. Dense woodlands were thinned, root-laced soil was broken by hand and plow, and log homes were raised with timber hewn from their own allotment.

Each season brought new demands: planting and harvesting, repairing tools, caring for livestock, preserving food, and preparing for the unrelenting winters of New England. Neighbors relied on one another for survival, and communal labor—whether constructing palisades, repairing bridges, or erecting meetinghouses—was part of daily life.

By autumn of that same year, Joseph became a member of the Windsor church, a necessary step toward full civic inclusion in a Puritan town where governance and religious life were deeply intertwined.

As Windsor evolved from a loose settlement into an organized community, Joseph became increasingly involved in public affairs. Within a few years, he was chosen to represent the town at the General Court in Hartford—Connecticut's legislative assembly. His inclusion signaled not just respect from neighbors, but a shared confidence in his judgment during a time when colonial law, property rights, and defense protocols were still in formation.

His name appears throughout town records: serving on juries, witnessing land transfers, participating in civil matters that helped establish a sense of order in an emerging colony. Alongside other key figures of Windsor's early years, he contributed to the frameworks—legal, agricultural, and social—that would endure beyond his lifetime.

Joseph remained in Windsor for nearly twenty years, during which he witnessed his children settle into households of their own, laying down roots that would carry the family name forward. His wife, Mary, died in 1652. He followed her in November 1658 at age 68. Though he left no formal will, his affairs were settled without conflict—an outcome that reflected the stability he had brought to both his family and his community.

2

Between Plow and Progress

By the early 1840s, the Loomis family, whose roots had long been established in this town, found themselves at a crossroads. The patriarch Josiah Loomis, now an established figure in Windsor, made the bold decision to head southward, away from the cold northern winds of New York to the warmer, yet uncertain soil of Virginia.

The world was changing, both in the North and the South, and Josiah, ever the visionary, recognized that Windsor's small-town rhythm no longer aligned with his ambitions or his family's future. The Industrial Revolution was gathering pace, and the question that had been circling his mind for some time now was no longer abstract: *Would the Loomis name become a relic of a bygone era if they stayed behind?*

He didn't want to wait and find out.

After arriving in Fairfax County, Josiah moved quickly to secure a place for his family. In March of 1842, after months of negotiation and travel, he finalized the purchase of 750 acres from Orlando Fairfax, scion of one of the state's most storied families. It was not merely a land transaction—it was a signal. Josiah had aligned himself with a region still steeped in patrician manners, but increasingly open to commercial ambition and social recalibration.

The land stretched across hills and creek-fed pastures, and he promptly subdivided it between his sons and their young families. Among them was his eldest, Nathan Loomis, a measured and steady man who had already begun carving out his own path long before the family's migration.

Nathan and his wife, Waitie Jenks (Barber) Loomis, built their life together in Oppenheim, New York, where between 1826 and 1840, they welcomed seven children: Mahlon, Eben, George, Ellen—who would later become the family's unofficial historian—Mary, Ellissa, and Collete. For these children, the Virginia countryside was a striking change from the rural pace of upstate New York. But here, in this new landscape, their formative years would take shape, balancing the old-world values of hard work with the rising influence of education and social progress.

Unlike the informal schooling, they had experienced back home—often little more than seasonal instruction interrupted by planting and harvest cycles—Nathan Loomis envisioned something more enduring, more expansive, for his children. While Josiah's generation had prized resilience and utility, Nathan believed that a fuller education could prepare his children not only to survive but to contribute meaningfully to a swiftly changing republic.

He sought for them more than rote literacy and the ciphering of sums. He wanted his daughters to interpret the

Constitution and his sons to read Tacitus alongside soil reports. Practical knowledge would remain—crop rotation, livestock management, the legalities of land—but Nathan aimed to widen the frame.

Virginia, though proud, still lagged in public instruction, particularly in the more rural precincts. Private academies did exist, but they were often costly, distant, and denominationally narrow. The standard he sought—a secular rigor grounded in both Enlightenment ideals and civic virtue—was, in many respects, unavailable. So, he resolved to create it himself.

This venture, fueled by his belief in the vital marriage of knowledge and community, quickly extended beyond the immediate needs of his household. Word traveled, as it did in those days, by saddle and supper table. Neighbors in adjoining tracts began sending their children, first hesitantly, then in steady numbers.

By the late 1850s, this little school had become more than an academic institution; it was a gathering place, a forum for civic exchange, and—perhaps most crucially—a symbol. In a land still divided by class, by geography, and increasingly by ideology, it stood for a quieter, more enduring proposition: that a community invested in learning could not easily be misled or broken.

And in time, the children educated beneath its pitched roof would carry that inheritance with them—into courtrooms, into commerce, into lives shaped not just by where they came from, but by what they had been taught to imagine.

However, Nathan's educational vision did not end there.

In 1851, his pursuits took a more unexpected turn when he was invited to join a scientific cohort in Boston—a group focused on recalibrating the very way Americans measured the world. The family relocated to West Springfield, Massachusetts, where Nathan became part of a pioneering effort led by mathematician Benjamin Pierce to establish an American prime meridian, challenging the long-standing reliance on Greenwich.

From their success, they created the *American Nautical Almanac*, a groundbreaking publication that would become essential for maritime navigation, offering detailed astronomical data for the guidance of sailors.

As the publication gained more prominence, Nathan and his colleagues' work took on national significance. In 1861, after several years of successful contributions in Boston, the organization was relocated to Washington, D.C., where it found a permanent home at the National Observatory—a place where its critical work could be further expanded and supported by the U.S. government.

The almanac was subsidized by a congressional appropriation, signaling the government's commitment to integrating scientific progress with practical, military, and maritime applications.

Though Nathan's name may not be widely recognized outside of scientific circles, his legacy lives on in the precise navigation systems that continue to shape our understanding of the world.

3

Star Charts and Scandals

With the almanac's national importance solidified, Nathan's son Eben Barber Loomis, following in his father's footsteps, was invited to join the team in Washington, D.C., in 1868.

Though still a young man, Eben's contributions to the field of astronomy had already begun to make waves. His early academic pursuits at Harvard had laid the groundwork for his eventual involvement in the almanac's work, and his keen interest in the celestial mechanics that governed the heavens made him an ideal addition to the team.

Once in Washington, Eben's role was clear: to push the boundaries of what was known about celestial calculations and refine the existing methods for more precise navigation. His work quickly gained respect within the scientific community as he brought a fresh perspective to long-established practices. While many of his colleagues were focused on technical accuracy, Eben's curiosity often drove him to explore new questions and hypotheses, opening up new avenues of research.

In the years that followed, Eben's influence on the field deepened, and his pursuit of new frontiers in astronomy continued.

In December 1889, he joined a U.S. Navy scientific team aboard the USS *Pensacola*, bound for the west coast of Africa. Their destination was Angola, selected for its optimal vantage point to observe a total solar eclipse—an event of profound interest to astronomers seeking to study the sun's outer atmosphere and the complex interplay of light, shadow, and motion that accompanied such rare alignments.

Once ashore, the team erected a temporary observatory with care and precision, their work unfolding in quiet anticipation. In an era without satellite imaging or digital forecasts, every calculation carried with it an immense weight of uncertainty.

Eben's hands had moved steadily over the delicate chronometers and lenses, aware that months of preparation would be judged by mere minutes of sky-darkened clarity. It was a big responsibility to shoulder, even for a man of his calibre. Yet, amid the tension, there was also a quiet exhilaration—a sense that he stood at the threshold of something rare.

As the eclipse drew near, time itself seemed to compress. Conversations fell to whispers, the air grew unnaturally still, and even the insects quieted as if in deference to the coming event.

Then, without fanfare, the world shifted.

A shadow swept over the landscape, the sky dimmed to an eerie indigo, and the sun became a narrow ring of fire. For a moment, science gave way to awe. Eben paused—just long enough to register the profound strangeness of it all—before turning back to his instruments.

He recorded temperatures, sketched the corona, noted the behaviors of the surrounding wildlife, his notes as calm and orderly as the man himself, even as the cosmos seemed to fold briefly inward.

When it was over, when the sunlight returned in a sudden flood and the spell was broken, the data had been captured. The mission, in all its fragility, had succeeded.

But for Eben, something less measurable remained.

In the aftermath of that shadowed noon, he felt a deeper conviction that the universe was not just a machine to be studied but a living rhythm to be felt. It was a belief he would carry with him on the long journey home—a sentiment woven through the pages of his book '*An Eclipse Party in Africa*', where he preserved not just the facts but the feeling of standing, however briefly, in the presence of the sublime.

Though his career was rooted in astronomy, Eben's soul seemed tethered elsewhere—to woodland paths, shifting light, and the quiet companionship of trees. His published volumes, *Wayside Sketches* and *A Sunset Idyll and Other Poems*, revealed a man whose thoughts wandered far beyond observatories. These weren't lofty verses detached from the world but grounded reflections drawn from long walks through Washington's quiet outskirts.

It was there, amid tangled brush and fading sun, that he walked along with Walt Whitman—a poet who was often hailed as the father of free verse and Henry Thoreau—a quietly rebellious philosopher and naturalist. Their conversations—sometimes spoken, sometimes silent—wove through topics as varied as politics, stars, and the way moss clings to stone.

While his accomplishments in astronomy and literature were considerable, the truth about his formal education was somewhat less remarkable. Eben attended Harvard's Lawrence Scientific School for just one term, a brief sojourn into formal academia that contrasted sharply with the image his family portrayed of him as a self-made scholar.

In the eyes of his wife, Mary Alden Loomis—a direct descendant of John Alden of the Mayflower—and daughter, Mabel Loomis Todd, Eben was a misunderstood genius, his accomplishments far greater than the world acknowledged. Their belief in his brilliance led them to craft a narrative that elevated him above the reality of his self-taught pursuits.

4

Hidden in the Margins

Eben's literary pursuits, though notable in their own right, never garnered the same recognition as those of his daughter, Mabel. As the first editor and publisher of Emily Dickinson's poetry, she was pivotal in bringing the reclusive poet's work into the public eye.

Though her relationship with Emily was based primarily on the shared bond of literature, their connection was not a simple one.

Mabel did not meet Emily until after her death, when her sister Vinnie reached out in 1887 with a series of letters, scraps of paper, and the quiet voice of a poet who, at the time of her death, was largely unknown to the world. Mabel worked tirelessly to transcribe these fragments and eventually earned her rightful place alongside T.W. Higginson's name on the title page of the first published collection of Emily's poetry in 1890.

However, while this triumph in the literary world was one for the history books, it was by no means without its personal toll.

Beneath the surface of Mabel's editorial triumphs, there was another, far more intimate and hidden relationship that would come to define much of her personal life—the affair with Emily's brother, Austin. It was an affair that spanned over twelve years, one that began in *secrecy* and remained concealed for much of her life.

It was only a visit her grandmother made to the Todds in 1884 that alerted Mabel's family to what was going on behind closed doors.

The elderly woman, ever perceptive despite her advanced age, quickly suspected that Mabel and Austin's relationship was far more than just a friendship. So, she summoned Mabel's parents, Eben and Mary Loomis, to Amherst, where they interrogated their daughter and Austin about the nature of their relationship.

John Walsh's book *The Brief Tragedy* recounts the details of this interrogation, noting the accusations made against Austin—namely, that he had not visited the Todd home as a guest would but instead slipped in the back entrance, often staying late into the evening with only Mabel for company.

Austin, in his typically eloquent manner, defended himself in a letter to Mabel.

He dismissed the accusations, assuring her that their relationship was pure and above reproach. "We are not to be frightened," he wrote confidently. "We are not of that cheap stuff. We are not afraid of the truth; our life together is as white and unspotted as the fresh driven snow. This we know, whatever vulgar-minded people, who see nothing beyond the body, may think or suspect."

Despite this bold defense, Austin also acknowledged the social reality they faced, admitting that they would have to "conform" to societal expectations and appearances, even if those standards were unjust and misguided.

The affair, however, was far from something that could easily be brushed aside.

Mabel, in particular, found it impossible to dismiss the affair's implications. Her reputation was tightly interwoven with the societal values of the time—values that demanded adherence to strict codes of propriety, especially for women. To be involved with a married man, particularly one in her close circle, carried with it not just personal shame but also the potential for irrevocable social disgrace. The idea of being discovered—of the affair spilling out into the public sphere—was a constant source of dread.

They took all measures to conceal it, but such things always had a way of getting out, much to her dismay.

In early 1885, a letter from her father reached her doorstep, written in what was described as "terrible" terms. The content of the letter remained a mystery, but its emotional weight was enough to cast Mabel into a prolonged state of depression. For weeks, she remained subdued, her spirits shattered by the realization that her parents—especially her father, whom she revered—were fully aware of the affair and were deeply troubled by it.

Despite the turmoil in her personal life, Mabel continued to work diligently on her literary projects, but the secrecy and guilt that accompanied her relationship with Austin never fully dissipated.

She longed for reconciliation, a way to bridge the gap between the woman she presented to the world and the woman she was forced to hide. Her journals reveal a deep yearning for peace but also an understanding that such resolution was unattainable. She could not undo the choices that had caused this fracture, nor could she escape the strain of living a life that was continually split in two.

In one particularly revealing entry, Mabel captured this tension in sharp, unvarnished language:

> *"Now that Emily's poems are actually out and my name on the title page, Sue (Austin's wife) rages more than ever. Why is a mystery to me, for they had the entire box of Emily's papers over there for nearly two years after she died, and Vinnie urging them all the time, even with fierce insistence, to do something about getting them published. But Susan is afflicted with an unconquerable laziness, and she kept saying she would, & she would perhaps until Vinnie was wild. At last, she announced that she thought nothing had better be done about it, that they would never sell— there was not enough money to get them out—the public would not care for them, & so on—in short, she gave it up. Then Vinnie came to me, and she begged me to copy and edit them."*

She had spoken her truth plainly—without embellishment or apology—but beneath the confidence of her words was a lingering ache. Editing Emily's poems had been a labor of devotion, a task she approached with reverence and precision. And yet, the bitterness surrounding their publication had become inseparable from her name.

Mabel's legacy, once tethered so closely to art and discovery, now floated in a *liminal space* between admiration and reproach. Critics and biographers often struggled—or refused—to separate her literary contribution from her private life.

This tension is perhaps best illustrated in John Walsh's book, whose interpretation became emblematic of the divided views surrounding her.

While Walsh did not paint Mabel in a wholly villainous light—he acknowledged her intelligence, charisma, and literary determination—his conclusion was unambiguous: her relationship with Austin, however passionate, brought lasting turmoil to the Dickinson family and irreparably complicated their history.

His title alone suggested a verdict—*brief passion, long regret.*

However, such over-simplification did little justice to the woman who was so much more than that. Her life was not a tidy parable about moral failure. To reduce her largely to the scandal was to overlook her profound role in shaping Dickinson's posthumous reputation.

After all, art does not cease to be art simply because it bears the marks of human flaw. Nor does the artist forfeit her worth for being the one who dared to shape it.

5

The Forgotten Genius

While Eben Loomis's name became synonymous with the quiet, careful nurturing of Mabel's literary success, and Mabel's own story became entangled in the passionate scandal, the Loomis family legacy was simultaneously being molded by yet another sibling—Mahlon Loomis.

Mahlon, born in Oppenheim, New York, in 1826, was a man whose life followed a course distinctly different from that of his siblings, yet whose achievements would quietly rival those of his more famous relatives. He was the sort of figure whose accomplishments, though remarkable, were seldom recognized in their time, and when they were, they often bore someone else's name.

In essence, it was a tragedy of the highest order—not of failure, but of obscurity.

From an early age, Mahlon exhibited the signs of a sharp and searching mind. He was a bright student, curious and methodical, with a particular fascination for the mechanics of the natural world. In classrooms and workshops alike, he showed a knack for precision, a tendency toward experimentation, and a calm self-assurance that set him apart.

This inquisitive nature eventually led him westward to Cleveland, Ohio, where he pursued the study of dentistry—a field that, at the time, was still in its rudimentary stages, straddling the line between trade and emerging science.

To support himself, he taught school, an early testament to his discipline and drive. But dentistry soon became more than a means of livelihood for Mahlon; it became his laboratory. It was there, among molds, metals, and mineral compounds, that his inventive spirit began to take root.

He noticed things that others didn't. He found details that eluded most. For him, it was all in the *intricacies.*

It was this relentless attention to the minute and the overlooked that led Mahlon to his first significant innovation. In the narrow space between necessity and curiosity, he began experimenting with alternative materials for dental prosthetics.

The dentures of those times were crude and uncomfortable, fashioned from porcelain and vulcanite—materials that were not only brittle and costly but also poorly suited to the delicate demands of the human mouth.

In them, Mahlon saw an opportunity. *A vision.*

Drawing on his keen understanding of material properties and an almost instinctive sense for practical improvement, he turned his attention to kaolin: a soft, chalk-white clay more often found on a potter's wheel than in a physician's toolkit.

It was, at first glance, an unlikely choice. But where others saw fragility, Mahlon saw potential.

The process was slow, stubborn, and unglamorous—yet he remained absorbed in it. Gradually, what began as an improbable experiment became something more: a method for shaping durable, natural-looking artificial teeth from the mineral plate.

It was, in its own modest way, a quiet revolution.

On May 2, 1854, he secured a patent for his method—a rare moment of formal recognition in a life largely lived out of the spotlight. Later, the same innovation earned him a patent in England, a mark of *distinction* few American dentists could claim.

His work took him to towns large and small—Earleville, Bridgeport, Philadelphia—places that offered patients but little in the way of kindred minds. And so he kept moving, drawn not by ambition alone, but by the distant pull of something yet unnamed. *His thoughts wandered.*

They knew not of preconceived lines that separated one field from another. They just ran rampant in the way they often did. However, this time around, they began to coalesce into something more tangible.

Electricity. In one of his earliest efforts, he set out to investigate whether electrical currents could influence the growth of plants. He arranged metal plates in the soil—one placed beneath the roots of the plant, the other at a short distance away—and connected them to a galvanic battery, allowing a continuous current to pass through the ground and the vegetation between.

Though the results were ultimately inconclusive—no consistent improvement in plant growth could be verified—it marked a *turning point.*

What intrigued him now was not what electricity could do, but where it came from. If the spark could be summoned from a lump of zinc and a bit of acid, why not from the earth itself? Or the sky? And so, he turned his gaze upward.

He began releasing kites into the air, their tails trailing long wires, delicate and humming. There was a logic to it: if lightning could arc across the heavens, surely the upper reaches of the atmosphere must carry a natural charge. What if, Mahlon wondered, that charged stratum could be tapped? What if it could be used—not just as a source of energy—but as a bridge between places?

In an entry dated February 20, 1864—preserved today among the holdings of the Library of Congress—Mahlon put pen to paper and wrote:

"I have been for years trying to study out a process by which telegraphic communications may be made across the ocean without any wire, and also from point to point on the earth, dispensing with wires."

He paused, then transcribed a fragment from six years prior—faint lines of thought, still forming, still circling the question that refused to leave him:

"...In 1858. I wrote a paper, which I transcribe here: I believe that as soon as something can be found to bear the same relation to the earth that a wire does, a telegraphic communication can be made without a wire. What relation does a wire bear to the earth? That is a question to be settled, and one which I must write more about another time, but it serves to conduct a distinct portion of fluid from point to point."

Soon, his experiments grew *bolder.*

In 1868, on two peaks in the Blue Ridge Mountains of Virginia—one at Cohocton, the other eighteen miles away—Mahlon prepared his most daring test yet. On each summit, he rigged a kite and wire, grounded the system with care, and connected it to a sensitive galvanometer.

From one peak, a message was sent—subtle, invisible, but unmistakable. The galvanometer on the distant mountain flicked its needle in reply. In Mahlon's own words:

> *"Equipment and apparatus at both stations were exactly alike. The time pieces of both parties having been set alike, it was arranged that at precisely such an hour and minute, the galvanometer at one station should be attached, or be in circuit with the ground and kite wires. At the opposite station, the ground wire already fastened to the galvanometer, three separate and deliberate half-minute connections were made with the kite wire and the instrument. This deflected, or moved the needle at the other station with the same vigor and precision as if it had been attached to an ordinary battery."*

Mahlon then turned to the second mountain. There, he repeated the setup: a kite, a wire, a galvanometer. But this time, when ready to "send," he touched the kite wire to the earth. It was a small action—nothing more than a hand brushing metal to soil—but it triggered a curious cascade.

By grounding the wire, he effectively drained a portion of the charge from the overlying air stratum. That subtle reduction—imperceptible to the eye—was enough to diminish the available charge at the other mountain's air-wire, causing the galvanometer needle there to deflect anew.

That change in deflection, Mahlon argued, was a *signal.*

Not just a phenomenon, not just an anomaly—but a message. It had moved silently across miles of open sky, with no wires to carry it. For the first time in recorded history, a human being had sent a signal over a distance without using wires.

Word of the experiment travelled slowly, carried not by headlines but through the quieter corridors of scientific interest. Mahlon had no cheering crowd at his side, no government grant waiting in the wings. But among the few who had witnessed the demonstration—Congressmen, curious naturalists, and skeptical scientists—there was an uneasy murmur.

If this were true, it would change everything.

In the weeks that followed, Mahlon wrote and rewrote accounts of what had occurred atop those peaks. He scribbled diagrams in the margins of old letters, drafted affidavits from those present, and sought support not just in spirit, but in dollars.

A group of Boston investors showed early enthusiasm, pledging capital to further the work. But the Panic of 1869—what came to be known as *Black Friday*—swept through the markets with ruinous force, and the backers quietly withdrew.

Hope flickered again two years later in Chicago, where a syndicate of bankers expressed interest in underwriting his continued research. Days before anything could be finalized, the Great Fire tore through the city, leveling not just buildings but the financial prospects of nearly everyone in them.

Still, Loomis pressed on.

By 1870, his efforts reached Washington, and a bill was introduced in Congress to incorporate the Loomis Aerial Telegraph Company and appropriate $50,000 to support his further experiments. It was a bold request from a largely self-taught man, operating with crude instruments and grand ambition. The idea, to many, sounded ludicrous.

During the congressional debate over his proposal, one senator acknowledged the strangeness of the idea—but with a notable caveat.

"It is as absurd as anything I ever heard," he admitted, *"except for the invention of Morse."* He went on: *"When the electric telegraph was first introduced, everybody agreed it was the most absurd thing that could be conceived. We know what that invention is now, and I am in favor of giving this poor fellow a chance and seeing if he can do something..."*

The bill passed the House in May of 1872, then the Senate in January of the following year. President Ulysses S. Grant signed it into law. But the $50,000 appropriation Loomis had hoped for never materialized.

He had come close—*unmistakably close*—to turning his private experiments into a national project. But the timing was cruel. Every time he took a step forward, fate sent him reeling back with blows he ultimately could not recover from.

Without funding, the work ground to a halt. What might have become the first wireless communication system in the world was left to gather dust on shelves.

*****

Nearly three decades after Mahlon Loomis sent signals between two mountain peaks, another man stood on the shores of the Adriatic, raising wires into the air.

By the time Guglielmo Marconi began his experiments in the 1890s, the world had changed. Electrical science had matured. Instruments now existed that Loomis had never seen—tools like the coherer and electrolytic detector, which could capture and interpret the fleeting waves that rippled through the atmosphere. With these, Marconi could measure what Loomis could only sense.

Mahlon had worked without precedent. His "aerial telegraph" had no school, no method, no blueprint. He had discovered that a wire suspended in the air could disturb another at a distance—had shown it, again and again—but he lacked the means to isolate what, precisely, moved between them.

Marconi, in contrast, arrived when the world was ready to understand. His results could be plotted, repeated, and applauded. He became the face of wireless communication—its father, as history would come to call him.

While Mahlon's work remained a curiosity—brilliant, perhaps, but unproven.

In his dedicatory address, Dr. Elisha S. Loomis—the family historian and an advocate for his relative's legacy—spoke with measured conviction on the matter: *"While we admit that Marconi put wireless telegraphy upon a business footing, we claim that, had Congress supported Dr. Mahlon Loomis when he appealed to it for financial aid, these United States could now claim the honor of this world-famous discovery, for the system of Dr. Loomis involves every principle claimed to be of more recent discovery."*

Mahlon Loomis died in 1886—his final years marked by a quiet obscurity that stood in stark contrast to the scale of what he had attempted.

He did not live to see the radio towers that would one day rise from coastlines and mountaintops. He never witnessed a signal crossing oceans or voices carried invisibly through the air. The world he left behind had not caught up with the one he had *envisioned.*

Retired Commander Thomas Appleby, of Washington, D. C., and George M. Applegate, of Oxford, N.J., also brought this to attention in their book:

"As has been mentioned, it is regrettable that the pioneering work of Mahlon Loomis has not been recognized to any extent by either the state or the national government, other than one or two roadside plaques where his memory is recalled in his honor. Only very few historians of early wireless are at all familiar with his work."

They further added:

"It is hoped that the neglect and omissions of this man's work are in the process of being corrected by a program now underway which may result in official and popular recognition of this American genius."

By the mid-1960s, nearly eight decades after Mahlon Loomis's quiet death, a campaign launched primarily by individuals outside the Loomis family aimed to secure this long-overdue recognition. But despite the group's dedication, their pursuit fell short. The broader acknowledgment they had hoped for—the kind that would place Loomis alongside names like Morse or Marconi—remained elusive.

Still, their work was not without consequence.

Thanks in part to these advocates, a small but enduring gesture materialized in Virginia. Dr. William Hodgkin, one of the central figures in the recognition campaign, took it upon himself to preserve what he could of Mahlon Loomis's legacy. He meticulously collected papers, fragments of correspondence, and surviving records, eventually depositing them with the Library of Congress.

Hodgkin was also instrumental in the placement of a state historical marker along State Road 7 at Bluemont, Virginia, close to the mountain where Loomis had launched his kites and glimpsed the future.

Within the records Hodgkin helped preserve, a more personal dimension of Loomis surfaced—one etched not in patents or petitions, but in the recollections of those closest to him. Chief among them was George Loomis, Mahlon's younger brother, who stood beside him during his final days and became the unofficial custodian of his memory.

In a letter to their sister Mary, George revealed the emotional toll of sorting through Mahlon's effects. Among the remnants were several of his brother's diaries. Two of them, George admitted, he destroyed—unable to bear the despair they contained. They chronicled a time of deep poverty, when Mahlon, once a figure of promise, had resorted to selling off *"the better parts of his wardrobe"* in order to eat. George found the writings too painful to preserve and unfit for others to endure.

Yet, not all was desolation.

In a separate letter to Acsha Loomis, Mahlon's estranged wife, George captured a poignant final exchange. *"He was conscious to the last, though sinking,"* he wrote. *"And suddenly, after being more or less quiet, he looked up, sat up in bed and quite loudly and clearly, grasping my hand with superhuman strength said, 'George, it is all right,' and lay back with utter serenity and joy in his face."*

In the end, there were no accolades, no parades, no inventions bearing his name—only a soft-spoken farewell and a final grip of the hand. But in that gesture, steady, deliberate, and full of clarity, was the essence of Mahlon Loomis himself.

A man of unpolished means but *staggering vision*. One who persisted when no one was watching. Who *dreamed* aloud into a skeptical world, and when the doors closed, kept building in silence.

6

A Portrait in Prose

Among the Loomis siblings, certain names echoed in public spaces—etched into patents, legislative records, or civic contributions. Others, like Collette's, remained pressed between the pages of private journals, scarcely audible beyond the walls of the family home.

Yet within those quiet entries, something rare endured: a sister's voice unclouded by *ambition*, alive with observation, affection, and startling clarity.

While brothers pursued invention, enterprise, and reform, Collette turned inward—recording not progress, but presence. Her life, though cut short at twenty by rheumatoid arthritis, was rendered vivid in the ink of her own hand.

Her journals spoke in the quiet cadences of daily life—sunlight falling through a parlor window, the arrival of a neighbor's carriage, the scent of fresh bread cooling on the sill. Beneath those gentle textures, however, lay something richer—a keen sense of emotional attunement, a private wit that flickered through her descriptions, and a devotion to her sister that anchored even the most ordinary of entries. And at intervals, the tone would shift: a sudden note of pain, a fleeting dread, a question left unanswered.

In these unguarded lines, the full breadth of her inner world gathered—fragile, perceptive, and quietly luminous.

"Tuesday, February 7, 1860 Springy morning - can almost hear the bluebirds, robins, and bobolinks.

Afternoon - D. called he goes to Boston tomorrow - he spoke of calling for me this evening to attend the lecture, but I shall not expect him.

Afterward - yes D. called and we went to the lecture. I heard Henry Ward Beecher and liked him very immensely - I was delighted with Henry Ward, I like him. Everyone did. The hall was chock full."

The way she chronicled her thoughts—a mix of anticipation, mild disappointment, and eventual satisfaction—spoke to a groundedness and resilience in the face of the mundane, and a deep appreciation for the meaningful, if sometimes fleeting, experiences that life offered.

"Sunday, December 23rd, 1860

Good sleighing which we despaired of yesterday because of the unceasing rain, which at last, was made snow. Father and Nellie (Ellen) at church. Mr. Hawks's feeds today I believe. He called here on the day of Henry Squires funeral and talked in a sympathetic manner about the 'early dead' in an enthusiastic manner about the secession movement and in an indignant way upon slavery - but he thought everything was 'squaring around for the best and that God was at the bottom of the great national mess.' We didn't quarrel at all about that or anything else."

By December, a subtle shift in Collette's tone became apparent when compared to her earlier February entry. What had once felt light and whimsical—a simple recounting of an evening's lecture and the joy of hearing Henry Ward Beecher— had evolved into a more thoughtful, even measured reflection.

Her musings about Mr. Hawks, though still written with a clear, direct hand, were tinged with the complexity of a nation in turmoil. She recounted his passionate views on secession and slavery without engaging in conflict, choosing instead to observe, as if to reflect on the growing dissonance around her, yet still maintain a distance from the discord. It was as though Collette, amidst the unraveling storm of her country, held her thoughts close, sharing them only in fragments that captured her acute awareness of the shifting tides.

"Wednesday, January 11, 1861

At Mr. B's. Pleasant afternoon with Mrs. Bowles and the children Mrs. B. mends stockings. The children show picture books. 'The New and the Old', by J.W. Palmer. 'The Professor'. Conversation with Miss Estay upon Charlotte Bronte, H. W. Beecher, and so on. Misty, rainy, and damp."

In Collette, there was a deep, unassuming richness found in the details, in the people around her, and in the moments that others might overlook.

One could envision the quiet satisfaction Collette might have felt had she known that, more than a hundred years later, the Brontës' novels would still captivate the imaginations of readers—that their works, which once held such meaning for her, would continue to inspire admiration for their depth and intricacy.

She would have been assured of the power of literature—*power of words*—that she had always believed in and held close to her heart. She would have found in her own musings a form worth greater appreciation.

If only she had known, Collette would have gauged her worth with improved accuracy. For she was nothing short of *extraordinary*—sensitive, discerning, and unafraid to linger in thought.

"Thursday, January 17, 1861 At last it befell that the weather grew colder and the icicles hang from the encrusted trees and the snow clings to the icicles and we know that the Lord has spared us the January thaw and suffered the sleighing to remain yet a little longer. George has gone to S. He expressed the very abolitionist desire this morning to get some real Yankee machinist to invent a machine to sink South Carolina with. Nellie is cooling snaps and otherwise proving herself an ornament to society and the cake business - Eliza is sanctioning by usage the practice of eating hot cookies, paring apples, and laughing."

The deepening of winter brought with it an added density to Collette's words—a maturing tone that matched the heaviness of the season. The entry folded national tensions into the intimate corners of family life—George's acerbic quip about South Carolina underscored the urgency of the times, yet the day unfolded with the same familiar rhythm of baking, conversation, and shared laughter.

Within her lines, the domestic and the historical existed side by side, neither overpowering the other. The calm of the interior world persisted, even as the outer world inched toward rupture. Collette's words preserved both—the innocence of small joys and the quiet thrum of something vast and irreversible approaching just beyond the edges of routine.

As she drew near her death, her entries took on a more poignant edge. She fought to keep any semblance of her past self, but if one dared read between the lines, they could decipher the nuance her feelings held.

"Saturday, March 2, 1861 Dark muddy, sleighing on the decline. Dr Stickney called this morning. Did not lance my foot, so I expect to die—am settling up my affairs—taking the good of the apples while I last, and reading the Republican, I play a little upon my 'pinany.'"

She faced physical pain with a kind of wry theatricality—resigned, but never entirely subdued. The visit from the doctor offered little in the way of relief, and yet she continued on, layering her daily routine with understated defiance. There was a clear effort to draw light from the ordinary—reaching for a piano key, leafing through political pages, savoring the sharp sweetness of winter apples.

It was in these moments, faced with limitations and uncertainty, that her spirit became most vivid. Even as her world seemed temporarily reduced, she remained attentive to the *quiet joys* still within reach, determined to hold onto them.

By her lived example, Collette shaped a philosophy: one could still claim moments of beauty, even as the body ached or the weather disappointed. Illness, uncertainty, or isolation did not negate the worth of a day. There was always something to hold: a conversation, a book, the flicker of candlelight against a windowpane. To notice it, to acknowledge it even briefly, was an *act of defiance* against despair.

In that sense, she remained defiant till the end.

Collette passed away on April 11, 1861, at the age of twenty.

That same day, her sister Nellie—*Ellen*—turned to her diary, reaching for verse to make sense of the loss. She knew that was what Collette would have wanted.

"My darling kitten died—'Her high-born kindred came and took her away from me and shut her up in a sepulcher, in the kingdom by the sea' – Poe"

Poe's lines spoke not only of death but of a departure that seemed inevitable for a soul like Collette's—one too rare and radiant to remain in a world bound by time and suffering. The metaphor of a "sepulcher, in the kingdom by the sea" hinted at a resting place where her brilliance would continue, where her spirit would transcend the ordinary, unconfined by the limitations of the earthly realm.

It was a farewell befitting her, for her light was never meant to dim, but to be carried on by the words that now marked her absence.

Part 2
The Parsons Family

"Col. Henry Chester Parsons was a leading pioneer in Virginia's wonderful development, so much of which is evident today as his dreams continue to come true. He was a man of waring foresight and prophetic vision."

—Green Lee Lecther

1

The Making of a Cavalryman

Long before the street bore his name, before the fields of St. Albans bent to his plow, Jethro Parsons carved a quiet *legacy* into the northern Vermont soil.

He was not a man of spectacle, nor one to leave behind a trail of letters or proclamations. Instead, his story lingered in the furrows of land he tilled, the sturdy generations that followed, and the horses that thundered across the family's acreage.

Born on October 29, 1811, Jethro came of age in a world that demanded more than it explained.

Expectations were clear, even if reasons were not—work hard, tend the land, provide for kin. He met these demands with quiet persistence, cultivating a life that spoke more through deeds than declarations. Alongside his wife, Comfort, he raised four children—Henry, John, Warren, and Katherine—on the same land he worked with unspoken reverence.

Among the many tasks that shaped their days—mending fences, hauling wood, gathering eggs—it was their care and affection for horses that stood out. The children spent long hours with them—riding bareback through dew-soaked fields, brushing manes to a sheen, and whispering secrets into warm necks.

Their bond with the animals gave color to a life otherwise ruled by necessity. It revealed a softness behind the work, a *freedom* that could not be plowed under.

Though little survives in record about Jethro Parsons—beyond the land he owned and the street that now bears his name—the measure of a man is not always found in what is written. Sometimes, it lives on in the soil he left behind, and in the children who learned, by his side, how to listen to the land.

Then came Henry.

Born on September 26, 1840, he was the eldest amongst his siblings and knew from a very young age the significance of discipline and determination. Like the others, he was no stranger to the rigors of farm life—but there was a keenness in him, a *thirst* for knowledge that led him from the family homestead to the University of Vermont.

By the spring of 1861, the nation had split.

The Confederate bombardment of Fort Sumter signaled the start of the Civil War, and across the country, young men weighed loyalty against fear, idealism against obligation.

Henry Parsons was then deeply immersed in studies, far from the bugle calls and drilling fields that now began to define the landscape of his generation. Unlike many of his peers, he did not enlist immediately. He watched from Burlington as newspapers printed casualty lists and his classmates joined Lincoln's early call for volunteers.

He seemed detached.

That was until younger brother, John Hains Parsons, enlisted with the 1st Vermont Infantry for a three-month term. That was when the war solidified in his mind. Still, he did nothing. He stayed behind with the rest of his family and tried to continue on with his usual routine.

Yet, none of them could avoid the painful uncertainty that dawned on them. They didn't know what the future had in store for John. They half-expected him to come back in a coffin.

However, when his initial term expired in August 1861 and he returned home, a semblance of normalcy washed over them. The tension in the Parsons household slowly began to ebb, but the looming presence of the conflict was never far from their minds.

Come the summer of 1862, the call to serve had become impossible to ignore.

John, though his return from the 1st Vermont Infantry had been a welcome reprieve, had already made his choice. He re-enlisted, this time with the 1st Vermont Cavalry.

His decision was the final push Henry needed.

Henry had been hesitant, unsure of his place in this larger conflict. He had always prided himself on his intellect, his capacity for reasoning, and his preference for peaceful solutions. But the urgency of the moment was undeniable. He could no longer remain distant, watching from the sidelines.

So, with a sense of purpose now steering him, Henry made his move.

He returned to St. Albans and began recruiting men from the town, calling on his childhood friends, the neighbors, and the men he had once worked alongside on the farm. His natural leadership was evident; soon, he had gathered an entire company, all willing to join him in the fight.

On September 18th—just one day after the smoke cleared over Antietam—Henry was officially commissioned as captain of Company L, 1st Vermont Cavalry. The timing was no coincidence. The bloodiest single day in American military history had laid bare the war's brutal reality, and the Union was in desperate need of capable men to lead fresh troops.

And Henry had long since proved his *worth*.

The train ride south was silent, save for the occasional clink of gear or the muffled sound of conversation—soft, almost respectful, as each man faced the reality of what lay ahead. They were heading into the heart of the conflict, but the specifics of their future were still unknown.

War, beyond the glossy newspaper headings and detached casualties, was something else entirely. It had a scent—damp wool, charred wood, the copper tang of rusting iron. It had a texture—mud that clung like guilt, wool uniforms that chafed in the midday heat, the coarse feel of leather reins worn smooth by anxious hands. It moved not as an idea, but as a presence— quiet and waiting, heavy in the lungs, crouched just beyond the tree line.

By the time Company L disembarked, the autumn fields had turned brittle underfoot. They arrived in a countryside frayed by movement—wagon ruts carved deep into the clay roads, trees stripped bare not by season but by fire, and fences broken not by weather but by men. Not quite the greeting they had expected.

Yet, they had to *tread on.* By the close of winter 1863, before the fields thawed and the trails turned impassable with spring mud, Captain Henry Parsons had already logged months in the saddle, guiding Company L through the sinews of a conflict still escalating.

Their journey through the previous campaigns had been largely uneventful, at least by the cruel arithmetic of war. There were no columns of dead to bury, no cavalry charges lost to disaster—only the steady toll of exhaustion, cold, and time.

Yet the absence of bloodshed did not mean the absence of strain. The roads were long and rutted, and the men—most barely out of adolescence—bore the growing weight of a war that rarely explained itself. Henry, more than many, felt the imbalance.

He led well, but in quiet—He watched, he noted. He *wrote.*

The war, for all its clamor, had not yet consumed every hour. So, whenever the lull fell over them, Henry would seize the opportunity and write to his mother. The letters had always been a duty—an obligation to remind her he was still well, still serving. They had been one-way communications, his thoughts and experiences neatly packaged and censored before they even left his hand. However, the letter sent in March of 1863 was different.

In this letter, Henry could no longer keep the weight of it all at bay. He spoke of the devastation, not just of men but of the land itself, how it had been altered, scarred, and twisted by the violence. He had witnessed entire fields reduced to ash, homes left to crumble, and families ripped apart by the war. The tone of the letter shifted—there were no more reassurances or stoic updates. There was only the *raw truth*, laced with the grief he could no longer hide.

Along with the letter, he enclosed a poem titled *Musings*. Even though it was far from a polished composition, it conveyed the deep sorrow that had taken root in him.

"I sat by my tent fire tonight, Mother, And I thought of the dear ones at home, Of the past with its promise so bright, Mother, Of the present so shrouded in gloom.

Of war — with its terrible facts, Mother, Of the mourning which fills the whole land Of the drama this army enacts, Mother With its phases so sad — are they grand?

I thought of the hearths and the hearts, Mother That a year hath enveloped in woe I thought of the dark gulf that parts, Mother The now, from the twelve months ago.

Of ten-times ten thousand laid low, Mother Of "mountains of grief" raised on high, Of the torrents of life blood that flow, Mother Oh, when will the channel be dry?

What I have seen of what has been And what is being done—The terrible waste The terrible blast The lands most terrible doom—Were enough to move a heart of stone Or make a soulless nature groan —"

The poem did not name battles or casualties. It did not preach or plead. But its sorrow was unmistakable—a quiet elegy from a man who had once believed that purpose might soften the cruelty of war, and who now knew better.

2

No Rest for the Weary

The days had bled together in a slow, creeping passage of time, each one indistinguishable from the last—until the day Henry had dreaded arrived, uninvited, at his doorstep.

He had sensed it before it came—not in the way a scout reports movement or a sentry hears hoofbeats in the dark, but in the subtler shifts that only a soldier seasoned by hardship could detect.

Cards lay untouched, pipes went unlit, conversations dried to murmurs.

Henry had moved through the camp with the weight of foreknowledge pressing down on his spine. It wasn't superstition—it was something more grounded, more earned. A pattern he had come to recognize: the sudden abundance of stillness, the heightened attention to the mundane. He had seen it before, on smaller scales, in minor conflicts that had still managed to leave major wounds.

And now, it was all around him again, coalescing like storm clouds over dry earth.

It was April 1st, 1863. The Confederates had moved swiftly, methodically—emerging from the tree line with merciless coordination. They weren't probing, they weren't bluffing; this was a strike, sharpened and premeditated.

The field, bordered by brittle hedgerows and churned clay, became a *snare.*

Company L was overwhelmed. It happened with the clarity of a nightmare: horses panicked, riders thrown, muskets fired in panicked succession, the acrid smoke curling into every crevice of vision. Orders shouted by Henry dissolved into the chaos, muffled by the percussion of volleys and the din of retreat. It was not a stand, but a rupture—an unraveling of cohesion, a scattering of bodies and strategy alike.

By the time the dust began to settle, the ledger of loss had been etched.

Twenty-nine of his men were dead or grievously wounded, crumpled among the wreckage of saddle tack and spent cartridges. Eighty-two others had been taken—rounded up like livestock, their captors grim and unsmiling. Ninety-five horses, too, were lost—a depletion as strategic as it was symbolic.

Henry stood amid the remnants—boots sunk into the clotted soil, face lined with ash and fatigue. The field bore no glory, only evidence: shattered canteens, slashed bedrolls, and the torn insignias of men who would not return.

This was no skirmish to be forgotten in the tide of reports. It was a reckoning. A turning point not of war's progression, but of Henry's own quiet descent into disillusionment.

The next morning arrived, but not with the promise of renewal—only with the sound of crows circling above a field too quiet for the season.

Henry had not slept. There was no space left in his mind for rest, only an aching litany of names he had not yet written to the families.

What haunted him most was not the violence itself, but how ordinary it had become. The way the line between life and death had blurred—how a man could laugh with a tin cup in hand one moment, and lie faceless in the dirt the next.

But war didn't pause for mourning.

Within days, orders came. They were to ride north—toward Pennsylvania, where Confederate movement was rumored, and the stakes felt suddenly heightened. Henry rode with the Army of the Potomac's Cavalry Corps, his unit tucked within the long, snaking column that advanced over roads rutted from storms and the weight of artillery.

The air grew warmer with each passing mile, spring deepening into early summer. Along the roadsides, wildflowers had begun to nod their heads in careless bloom—yellow yarrow, blue phlox, white daisies—all untouched by the slow machinery of war that crept past them. To Henry, the sight was almost jarring in its indifference.

Beauty persisted, even when men didn't.

For days, the landscape unfurled as though trying to soothe them—soft hills, open fields, the occasional distant farmhouse, shuttered and watching. There was less talk now. Less laughter around the fires at night. April had drawn a line, and many had crossed into a quieter version of themselves.

And then, on the morning of June 20th, the silence was interrupted.

Hanover rose over the horizon like a dream half-remembered—brick facades, steeples, and bunting already hung from windowsills. They had reached it at last. The town lay waiting, unaware of what was coming.

For a few miraculous hours, the soldiers were welcomed as heroes. There were garlands strung between lampposts. Women brought platters of food. Boys shadowed the regiments, wide-eyed with admiration.

Henry, riding farther back in the column, watched General Kilpatrick enter at the front with his staff—regal and unflinching. Close behind came a figure impossible to miss: General George Armstrong Custer, fresh-faced at twenty-three, with curls that caught the sunlight and a uniform more suited to a portrait than a battlefield. He led his brigade like a prince entering a court—flamboyant, but unshakably in command.

For Henry, it was almost disorienting. He had expected skepticism, even fear—but instead there was joy. Color and music after so many months of grey and silence. For a brief and dangerous moment, he let the warmth of welcome soften him.

"Once more we were in 'God's country, and the hard, hot plains of the South were far behind. The green fields, yellow hillsides, orchards burdened with ripening fruits, comfortable

homes, great barns and grassier were on every side. There were no more fruitful or comfortable regions in the North, or in the world, than we looked down upon the morning of the 30th of June. The town of Hanover, a village with brick houses, broad lawns and shaded streets, welcomed us as deliverers. Flags waved everywhere. Bells were ringing. Hundreds of school children stood in the market square singing songs of welcome. The principal street was walled with tables burdened with food. In the cross streets came carriages bringing people and provisions from the country. Matrons and maidens and children ran with bread and milk, beer and pretzels. Dinners hot from the fires were brought to the tables and to the hungry, homesick army, it was a scene perhaps unsurpassed in all the marches of the war."

Henry had barely shaken the sleep from his eyes when the order came to mount. Word passed like wildfire: Confederate videttes had been spotted southwest of town, near Gitt's Mill. At first, it seemed nothing more than another probing scout, the kind that had grown almost routine. But by the time the troopers of the 18th Pennsylvania Cavalry reached the edge of the tree line, the air had already thickened—too quiet, too heavy with the smell of sunbaked oats and gun oil.

"Suddenly, a shell crashed through the buildings; then another, and a third."

The first shots cracked through the hedgerow. One man—a gray coat slumped in the saddle—toppled like a scarecrow. Then came the others. It was over fast. Twenty-five men from Company G were taken, just like that, bundled into the morning like hay into a cart.

"In a moment, the whole scene was changed. The population had vanished into the houses and hiding-places, and the army

hastily finished its repast in the deserted town. The rear-guard had been driven in, and came thundering down the street. Our ambulances had been captured, and the regiment had been defeated by a bold charge, led by Gen. Stuart himself."

J.E.B. Stuart had been pushing hard. His men had ridden through heat and hunger, delayed by rain-swollen creeks, clattering across Maryland like shadows with sabers. Stuart himself was a vision from another age—wide-brimmed hat pinned with a plume, beard neatly trimmed, boots gleaming in the sun.

There was a sense of theater to everything he did.

To Henry, it always seemed Stuart carried war like a flourish, the way an actor might a cape. But beneath the dashing posture was steel, and the glint in his eye was not for show.

It was just past midday when Stuart's vanguard reached Hanover. He came in hard, hoping to punch through the rear of the Union cavalry column—no delay, no rest, just fury.

And for a moment, he had it.

The town that had fed and cheered Union troopers mere hours before erupted in smoke and splinters. Cannon shells clawed through brick facades. A horse lay twitching near the bakery where Henry had tasted real bread for the first time in weeks.

But Henry wasn't there to witness Stuart's arrival. He was farther down, riding fast, responding to the crackling telegraph of panic that spread from the rear.

By the time he reached the center of town, the scene had unraveled into chaos. The streets, so recently thick with children's song, now rang with the slap of boots and the bark of field guns. Men scrambled to regroup. Ambulance wagons, briefly captured, were now lost entirely—horses run off, drivers missing. The bold Confederate charge had cleaved a seam through the Union line like a blade through canvas.

And yet—amid the wreckage, the resistance rose.

"Fortunately, Maj. Hammond, with a portion of the 5th N.Y., and Capt. Woodward, with a portion of the 1st Vt., occupied an elevated position in a cross street, where they could watch their opportunity and direct a counter-charge. They struck the head of the pursuing column, with its disordered ranks and spent horses, a fierce and resistless blow, cutting down the leaders and capturing men and horses. They so closely pursued Gen. Stuart himself that he barely escaped by jumping a fence and breaking through a garden thicket."

Henry would never forget what he saw then: Stuart's horse—sleek, black, foaming—clearing a fence at full gallop, the general hunched low against its mane, vanishing into a garden thicket behind a churchyard wall. It was not grace that saved him, but instinct.

The sun dipped low, casting long shadows down the alleys of (?). Smoke curled from the eaves. Horses stood heaving in their traces. And Henry, still gripping the reins, realized it had all shifted. Not just the skirmish—but the whole shape of things. Stuart, the great Confederate knight, had been delayed. The stars and maps had begun to realign.

*****

They rode again at dawn—through orchards and pasture, past barns half-burned and wells left open. The road east grew rougher, the sky heavy with heat. Union brigades fanned out like wings, converging on the hills ahead.

There, beyond the broken fences and scorched hedgerows, the Confederate cavalry had paused, but not prevailed. The order was swift: *forward*. And with it, the Union line surged—scattering the rebel pickets, reclaiming the road to Gettysburg.

Only later did Henry fully grasp the scale of what had transpired.

What should have been a clean arc northward—Stuart's intended sweep behind Union lines—had become a labyrinth of detours and delays. His men, once quick as foxes, now dragged through unfamiliar territory, flanked at every turn.

Colonel Samuel Alexander, a steely-eyed commander from the 1st West Virginia Cavalry, struck like a thorn from the shadows, his men riding hard through the dark, never giving Stuart a moment's peace.

On another flank, Colonel Henry Estes of the 1st Vermont Cavalry moved with the same quiet precision, keeping pace along narrow lanes and wooded creeks, denying the Confederates any chance to regroup or outrun them.

It was death by attrition—no great battle, just the slow, unyielding bite of pressure applied hour after hour.

The oppressive summer heat hung thick in the air, stifling and oppressive as the Union cavalry continued to advance toward Gettysburg. Tension swelled within the ranks, a quiet but unmistakable sense of foreboding that loomed larger with every passing mile. The horizon beckoned, but with it came uncertainty—a promise of confrontation and the uneasy knowledge that war had arrived at their doorstep.

As the column continued its march, they passed through the charming, yet now unnervingly tranquil, town of Oxford. Its cobblestone streets, lined with neat, whitewashed homes, presented a stark contrast to the anxious energy that permeated the air. What had once been a peaceful village now teetered on the edge of chaos, its residents gripped by an all-consuming fear of what was to come.

Henry's gaze swept over the town, which seemed suspended in an uncertain limbo between its former serenity and the impending maelstrom.

In the distance, the faint rumble of artillery fire reverberated, an eerie reminder that the war was no longer some distant specter—it was here, encroaching steadily upon them.

Henry would later recount the moment with a tinge of disbelief: *"The beautiful town of Oxford."*

But beauty had all but dissipated.

"Filled with people fleeing, panic-stricken, driving cattle and sheep with wagons loaded with their families and every living and portable thing. They also brought their wildest reports of disaster."

Rumors, fueled by the hysteria of the moment, had begun to circulate like wildfire.

Some claimed that the Union armies had been utterly routed, their forces decimated beyond recovery. Others spoke in hushed tones of the Confederate army marching on

Philadelphia, the city that had long been considered the cornerstone of the Union's identity.

To the terrified citizens of Oxford, the thought of Philadelphia falling was unthinkable. In their eyes, it was the citadel of the nation's spirit—its loss would be a devastating blow, a mortal wound to the heart of the Republic itself.

"Our armies had been defeated and destroyed. The rebels were already marching on Philadelphia, which to these people seemed to be the very citadel of the Nation."

By the time they left Oxford behind, the road had grown hushed. Here and there, Union scouts moved like ghosts through the brush, alert to every snapped twig and rustling leaf.

Henry tightened his reins. He could feel it—not in the way one senses weather or hears distant cannon—but in the marrow of his bones. Something irreversible was about to unfold.

As the 1st Vermont Cavalry pressed northward, dispatches reached them in fragments.

Stuart's cavalry—*confederate, elusive, once vaunted*—had faltered. His intended sweep behind Union lines had collapsed into a meandering, disjointed march through unwelcoming territory, pursued relentlessly by Federal brigades and harried by terrain he could not tame. The delay proved costly.

Lee had been left blind during the critical opening hours of the battle that now raged near Gettysburg.

3

Farnsworth's Charge

"Upon the request to reply to published statements," Henry wrote, *"I only undertook to give evidence of my own knowledge, but after consultation with surviving officers I have decided to attempt a general description of the charge and of the movements that preceded it."*

And in that quieter, but no less consequential war, Colonel Henry C. Parsons took up the pen.

What followed would become the definitive Northern account of Farnsworth's Charge—arguably the most disputed cavalry action of the war. Parsons was no historian by trade, but he understood the stakes. Truth, as he saw it, had been blurred by distance, pride, and the self-preserving narratives of generals.

So, he returned to the field in his mind, and with the same clarity and restraint that had marked his service, he set out to draw a true line across the page.

*****

On July 2nd, Henry's unit encamped south of the town, their bivouac pitched in the shadows of low hills streaked with smoke. Skirmishes erupted sporadically in the distance, the crack of rifle fire and dull percussion of cannon sounding like the throes of an angry earth. The mood in camp was tense—men moved with hushed purpose, tightening saddle straps, oiling pistols, speaking only when necessary.

No one slept well.

By first light on July 3rd, word spread that General Hugh Judson Kilpatrick had devised a plan. It was audacious in scope and questionable in merit: a mounted assault against the entrenched Confederate right near Big Round Top.

"Hood's division is turning our left; play all your guns; charge in their rear; create a strong diversion."

The landscape was wholly unsuited for cavalry maneuvers— steep, broken, densely wooded. Any frontal attack would be suicide. Colonel Elon Farnsworth, barely in his mid-twenties, newly commissioned and already revered for his composure under fire, protested.

"General, do you mean it?" he asked, his voice low and incredulous. "Shall I throw my handful of men over rough ground, through timber, against a brigade of infantry?"

But Kilpatrick did not flinch.

"A handful?" he replied, almost scoffing. "You have the four best regiments in the army!"

Farnsworth's face tightened. "You forget—the 1st Michigan is detached. The 5th New York, you've sent beyond call. I have nothing left but the 1st Vermont and the 1st West Virginia—

regiments already fought half to pieces." He drew in a breath, then added with restrained fury, "These are too good men to kill."

"Do you refuse to obey my orders? If you are afraid to lead this charge, I will lead it myself."

The words struck like a lash. Farnsworth flared. He rose in his stirrups, his broad shoulders squared, his face flushed with anger not of cowardice, but insult.

"Take that back," he growled, eyes narrowing beneath his campaign-worn kepi.

For a moment, tension coiled between them—a brittle silence held taut by pride and fury. The heat of the July afternoon seemed to pulse around them, cicadas droning in the distant woods, horses shifting restlessly beneath them. Then Kilpatrick's posture softened; the storm broke just slightly.

"I didn't mean it," he muttered, almost sheepishly. *"Forget it."*

Farnsworth's anger, too, subsided, but not without leaving something in its wake. When he next spoke, his voice was quiet but resolute, the voice of a man who had made peace with the cost of obedience.

"General," he said, "if you give the order—I will lead the charge. But you must take the responsibility."

Kilpatrick nodded, the gesture clipped but unmistakable. "I take the responsibility."

It was in this moment—on the cusp of a fateful charge—
that Henry observed them both closely, the image burning itself
into his memory with a clarity that would never leave him.

*"The two young generals at that moment in the shadow of the
oaks and against the sunlight, Kilpatrick with his fine gestures, his
blond beard, his soft hat turned up jauntily, and his face lighted
with the joy that always came into it when the charge was sounded.
Farnsworth, heavy-browed, stern and pale but riding with
conscious strength and consecration, two men opposite in every line
of character, but both born to desperate daring."*

That singular moment beneath the oaks captured the
essence of two leaders shaped by war—one who charged for
glory, the other who charged for duty. And in the final light
before the thunder of hoofbeats began, they stood as mirror
reflections of courage—divergent in spirit, but united in fate.

The cavalry was divided into battalions for the advance.
Henry was among those positioned to ride at the front. It was a
position not only of visibility but of terrible vulnerability. From
his vantage, he had a clear view of the terrain ahead and the
deteriorating situation around them.

*"Watson rode with me; General Farnsworth and Adjutant-
General Estes rode with Major Wells."*

While many of the other officers exuded an air of youthful
enthusiasm or fiery determination, Major William Wells was the
embodiment of composed experience. He had seen enough
action in the war to understand that there was little room for
bravado when lives hung in the balance.

"As the First Battalion rode through the line of our dismounted skirmishers, who were falling back, they cried to us to halt."

There was no time for hesitation. The battlefield was alive with movement, and the men pushed forward, not knowing what awaited them beyond the cover of the woods.

"As we passed out from the cover of the woods, the 1st West Virginia was retiring in disorder on our left."

The sight was disheartening—an unsettling reminder of the fragile nature of victory, how swiftly it could turn to defeat. Yet there was no time to dwell on the retreating soldiers or question their fate. The situation demanded action, and action was what they had come for.

Then, as if nature itself sought to add an element of surrealism to the chaos, a frantic horse came galloping toward them, its side bloody, its leg cruelly torn off by the blast of a cannonball. The beast appeared to be seeking refuge, its eyes wide with terror, as if driven by some primal instinct to find protection.

The fear didn't deter those going in the opposite direction. The Union men pressed on, their resolve unbroken, riding through the smoke and din of battle.

"We rode through the enemy's skirmish line across the fields, over the low fences, past the Slyder house, and down the road."

The very landscape around them seemed distorted by the chaos, the blinding sun above only amplifying the disorienting atmosphere. Captain Cushman, riding ahead, shielded his eyes with his hand, squinting into the distance as his voice rang out above the confusion:

"An ambuscade!"

It was a grim realization, but there was no turning back now.

They were upon the enemy before they could react—within thirty paces, too close for comfort. A deadly volley, described in Confederate reports as the decisive strike, was unleashed upon them.

However, contrary to what the reports claimed, the volley flew harmlessly over their heads. Though the enemy's fire was concentrated and deadly, not a single rider fell that day, defying the odds. The reports spoke of saddles emptied, of men struck down, but here, by some twist of fate, they survived. It was a stroke of luck that could not be explained, a mere whisper of fortune in a place where such things were rare.

Captain Jones, commanding the right flank of the 4th Alabama, later recalled the frantic moments that followed: *"I was ordered to face about to resist cavalry,"* he said, his voice steady, but marked by the intensity of the memory. *"We marched rapidly to the rear over the rocky terrain, and the Vermonters were upon us before we could even form ranks. They were within a few paces when we gave the order to fire."*

The enemy was upon them, and they had no time to properly respond. But when the smoke of battle lifted, only one horse had fallen—a testament to the ferocity and precision of the Union charge. Captain Jones turned to his men, incredulous at the turn of events, and asked the private beside him why he had not aimed at the rider instead of the horse.

The private's response was an unexpected one: "Oh, we'll get him anyhow; but I'm a hunter, and for three years I haven't looked at a deer's eye—I couldn't stand it."

Henry, close enough to observe the exchange with a growing sense of unease, sensing the mounting tension that crackled around them.

All around them, the cacophony of musket fire, hoofbeats, and shouted orders blended into a brutal symphony of *chaos*. Yet in the midst of it, Henry remained alert, his eyes sweeping the broken terrain for any sign of movement, any shift in the tide that might demand an instant response.

The unnerving calm that followed the Confederate volley was deceptive. Henry could feel it—an invisible pressure tightening across the ranks. The enemy had regrouped, and somewhere ahead, unseen rifles waited, sights fixed, nerves taut.

"Taken by surprise, they had shot over us; the next, a random volley, was effective. With the head of the column we cleared the wall at the right and formed under cover of the hill. The rear companies fell back and formed behind a cross fence and in the edge of timber. In the meantime, the most important movement of the day was being made."

Ahead, the Second Battalion, led by the indomitable Major Wells, began to move. It was a calculated sweep, a bold arc carved through fire and stone. They looked almost spectral—figures surging through dust and shadow, the banners snapping, sabers lifted, the thunder of hooves swelling as they charged along the base of Round Top. Their movement cut directly across the Confederate rear, disorienting the enemy ranks and severing their cohesion.

Simultaneously, Colonel A. W. Preston—an unflinching Vermonter who had already proven his mettle in earlier engagements—took command of the Second Squadron and part of the Third Battalion. His orders were clear: press forward toward Devil's Den, a place already infamous for its treacherous rocks and bloody fighting.

Preston's men descended a steep, broken slope at a careful trot, the horses slipping on loose stones, the line bending to the terrain's cruel whims. Dust, pungent with the smell of trampled grass and gunpowder, rose in choking clouds around them.

At the foot of the declivity, the column swung left. They passed close by a Union battery hammering out volley after volley, its gunners stripped to shirtsleeves and blackened with sweat and soot.

In the smoke and confusion, the battery's infantry support mistook Preston's riders for a Confederate force and unleashed a furious volley. Musket balls hissed and cracked through the air, shredding leaves and striking dangerously close, but the column pressed on without breaking.

Once past the worst of it, the column divided into three swift-moving parties.

One group swept out across the open fields and fell upon the rear of the Texas skirmish line. In the desperate tangle that followed, they captured part of the Confederate line as prisoners. A few among them, finding no resistance, pressed onward and rode straight through into the Union lines.

Nearby, disaster struck General Farnsworth.

His horse, frantic and exhausted, went down hard. Before Farnsworth could be trapped, a trooper dismounted under fire, thrust his own reins into the general's hand, and fled on foot into the rocks. Regaining a mount, Farnsworth, accompanied by Captain Cushman and a handful of others, turned back and galloped at full speed toward the point where they had first entered the battlefield.

Meanwhile, the situation demanded renewed action. Henry's squadron was ordered forward once again. As they moved, Confederate sharpshooters emerged among the rocks above, their muzzles flashing in the sun, sending a sharp, cutting fire down into the Union cavalry.

Henry wheeled his horse obliquely up the rocky incline, angling toward Major Wells's position. The column turned left sharply, threading between the scattered picket line and a low stone wall that stitched across the broken ground.

As they swung about, Corporal Sperry, riding at Henry's side, was struck down without a sound. Henry saw him fall out of the corner of his eye, but there was no time to stop. Part of his men peeled away, escorting prisoners rearward, even as the head of the column vaulted the wall and burst into the open field beyond.

Ahead, General Farnsworth—rallying to the sight of friendly horsemen—raised his saber high in the air and charged forward as if leading an army, though only a handful of riders remained at his side. At almost the same instant, the remnants of the First Battalion slashed their way through the 15th Alabama. The Confederate regiment, caught mid-maneuver and scrambling to form into line, offered little resistance before breaking apart under the ferocity of the assault.

Henry's squadron charged in the same general direction, but on the opposite side of the low wall that ran parallel with the slopes of the Round Top range. The two forces, though divided by the barrier, were no more than two hundred paces apart.

Amid the thundering charge, Henry glimpsed Sergeant Duncan.

"Sergeant Duncan, a black-eyed, red-cheeked boy, splendidly mounted, standing in his stirrups, flew past me with his saber raised, shouted, 'I'm with you!' threw up his left arm, and fell. My horse recoiled over his dead body, my men swept past, and I was for a moment alone on the field."

For an instant, Henry felt a bewildering stillness close around him, a stillness so complete it was almost offensive after the furious momentum of the charge. The air was thick with gun smoke and the sharp, stinging reek of black powder, but the battle sounds had seemed distant, muted, as if the earth had tilted and left him outside the normal bounds of movement and noise.

He became acutely aware of small, absurd details: the way his horse's flanks trembled beneath the saddle; the jagged tear along his left gauntlet where a bullet must have grazed it; the brittle snap of a dry weed underfoot. Somewhere behind him, a saber rang out against stone, a sharp, ringing clash that carried an almost musical clarity against the blood-warm air.

He knew, without needing to see it, that the enemy was *closing in.*

The shouting, half-triumphant, half-cautious, came from men who had not expected to catch a cavalry officer alive. The tone was almost pleading—*Surrender, damn you, don't make us shoot*—but Henry knew better than to mistake it for mercy. They were as scared as he was, and fear made the finger tighten faster on the trigger.

His body responded before his mind could catch up. He straightened in the saddle, lifting his saber high—not a gesture of desperation, but one of pure instinct, the ancient reflex of a soldier refusing to fall on his knees.

"A gun was planted against my breast and fired; my horse was struck at the same moment and broke frantically through the men, over the wall, and down the hill."

The blast that followed came with a flash of searing white.

A peculiar sensation bloomed in Henry's ribs—not pain exactly, but a prickling heat, like standing too near a forge. When he glanced down, the sight of blood soaking through the torn seams of his coat seemed absurd, almost theatrical.

He blinked hard, once, twice, but the image remained.

His horse, wide-eyed and wild with terror, plunged sideways, its powerful body carrying them both out of the closing noose. Rocks blurred past. He was dimly aware of Corporal Waller's horse drawing up beside him, of a hand reaching out, gripping his arm hard enough to bruise, anchoring him in the saddle.

Henry did not feel victorious. He did not even feel alive in the ordinary sense. He was *moving*, he was *breathing*, but a part of him had already been left behind in that circle of muskets, where a different ending had almost been written in an instant.

"As we rode on, he told me how Farnsworth and Cushman had fallen together."

Henry remembered the way Waller's voice carried over the horses—quiet but steady, as though trying not to disturb the dead. He didn't offer details right away, nor embellishment. Just the fact, lodged like a bullet: both men were down.

4

History Rewritten

The charge—so often dismissed later as reckless—was, in truth, neither aimless nor insane.

Henry Parsons knew the truth of what had transpired on the battlefield at Gettysburg. He had been there, leading his men through the confusion and carnage, his thoughts consumed by the brutal reality of the charge.

It was meant to be a diversion, nothing more.

General Farnsworth and his men had been ordered to ride deep into the Confederate lines, drawing fire and creating chaos ahead of the main movement. The mission was clear: to disrupt and confuse, not to triumph in a full-scale cavalry assault. They were to create an opening, not force one themselves. But as often happened in war, things went awry.

The ground was too uneven for a cavalry charge, and the Confederate defenses were too strong. Yet, despite the overwhelming odds, Captain Cushman, riding with Sergeant

Stranshan and the splintered remnant of Company L, had gone forward into the teeth of it. Watson's horse had gone down early, and the command had passed like a flame from hand to hand.

Some men fell back, dragging prisoners with them. Others were scattered, swallowed by smoke, or thrown by the churn of the fight. In the end, fewer than fifty remained—those with Farnsworth, still cutting their way forward into the depths of enemy lines.

Somewhere near the stony outcropping, hemmed in on all sides, his horse went down. Waller said he'd been shot several times—no one could tell which bullet had ended it. It had happened quickly, but without confusion. There had been no theatrics, no last cries. Only the kind of stillness that follows true violence.

Yet, the Confederate reports told a completely different story.

The Southern accounts, particularly those written by Colonel Evander M. Law and other Confederate officers, spun a version of events that made Farnsworth's death into an act of self-preservation. According to these reports, Farnsworth had been cornered by Confederate forces and, realizing that capture was imminent, had taken his own life rather than be taken prisoner.

"Farnsworth cried out a refusal to surrender, then fell dead. Rebel observers later claimed he had shot himself to end his agony."

The Confederate narrative, in its attempt to diminish Farnsworth's legacy, made no attempt to veil the scorn with which they viewed him, positioning his final moments as a tragic admission of weakness rather than courage. But the truth lay in the wounds.

When Farnsworth's body was at last recovered, it bore five mortal injuries—each to the torso and limbs, none to the head. Doctors Edson and Wood, who examined him with care and solemn precision, confirmed this plainly. There was no sign of suicide, no evidence to sustain the slander.

That was when the origin of the *myth* came into perspective.

At the time of his fateful ride at Gettysburg, Farnsworth had just been promoted to brigadier general—his commission dated June 29th, 1863, merely four days before his death. But in the chaos of the campaign, the formal trappings of rank were out of reach. Uniforms did not arrive by courier on time, and so, on the field, practicality took precedence.

In a gesture of respect and camaraderie, Major General Alfred Pleasonton, Farnsworth's superior, shared from his own wardrobe. Farnsworth rode into action wearing Pleasonton's tailored blue coat, which bore a single star upon the collar—a token both of temporary necessity and lasting regard. On his head, instead of the regulation kepi, he wore a soft, wide-brimmed black hat, likely also Pleasonton's.

Cushman, who had accompanied Farnsworth into the maelstrom that day, was also struck down—wounded grievously in the face during the final moments of the charge.

He had been a striking figure on the field, dressed in an unusual white duck "fighting jacket" trimmed in yellow braid, a gift from a woman who had sewn it by hand and claimed no rebel bullet could pierce it.

When Henry had scoffed at the garment earlier that day, Cushman only smiled and pinned a silk handkerchief to the brim of his cap, letting it hang down like a veil against the heat. *"It may be a good day to test magic mail,"* he said lightly.

When Farnsworth fell, Cushman kept fighting, emptying his revolver until he too was brought down. He collapsed near the general, bloodied and motionless, his unusual attire catching the eye of the advancing Confederates.

It was this vivid image—of a man in white, wounded but defiant—that Southern observers later described. In multiple Confederate accounts, they recalled a Union officer wearing a light linen coat and bearing a notable hare-lock, who refused to surrender and fought to the last with a pistol before ending his own life. This man, they believed, had been General Farnsworth.

But it was not. It was Cushman they had seen.

The confusion was understandable. The clothing matched, the location matched, and Cushman's brave stand made an impression. Yet the man they had mistaken for the fallen general survived the night, though unconscious and disfigured. He lingered a while longer—long enough to correct no myths, to seek no attention—before dying in a subsequent engagement.

Farnsworth's commission had remained among Pleasonton's field papers during the days of movement and confusion, never reaching the young general in life. So he had fought and died without ever formally receiving the rank he had earned.

And that was a *tragedy* of the highest degree.

Kilpatrick, who should have stood in defense of his fallen subordinates, uttered only tepid platitudes for Farnsworth—words that felt more like a dismissal than a eulogy.

"For the honor of his young brigade and the glory of his corps, he gave his life. We can say of him, in the language of another, 'Good soldier, faithful friend, great heart, hail and farewell."

By failing to mention Farnsworth's courage in the face of certain death, Kilpatrick unwittingly reinforced the damaging rumors that Farnsworth had chosen to end his own life.

This was just one example of Kilpatrick's broader pattern of questionable decisions.

His leadership was often seen as erratic, his decisions impulsive, and his judgment clouded by an almost reckless ambition. Though he was known for his daring and boldness, these same qualities often led him to make dangerous choices with little regard for the consequences.

The same was true for Farnsworth's charge.

Kilpatrick had been entrusted with significant autonomy by General Pleasanton, a level of discretion that allowed him to make key decisions on the battlefield. However, this freedom was squandered through a series of tactical blunders that would prove disastrous for his men. His overconfidence and a misguided sense of strategic genius led him to make commands that defied basic military logic.

The first of these was glaring in its miscalculation. Kilpatrick, in an effort to press forward and gain an advantage, made the fatal error of sending men on foot when they should have been mounted, and vice versa.

Riders, accustomed to the swiftness of their horses, were made to march on foot, their advantage in mobility stripped away. Conversely, men on foot, who could have been better used in strategic positions, were sent to mount horses, forcing them into conditions for which they were ill-prepared.

Yet Kilpatrick, either too eager or too caught up in the momentum of battle, deployed his men in ways that left them vulnerable and exposed. He failed to properly utilize the strength of his cavalry and, in the process, failed to fulfill his mission.

In an attempt to rectify his mistake, he sent Colonel Richmond's West Virginians into an open valley—a move that would prove catastrophic.

Kilpatrick's thinking was flawed from the very start: he believed that if he could provoke a battle, draw the Texas regiment into the open, and break their lines on the mountain, Meade's infantry stationed on Round Top could then drive the enemy back into the valley, where Kilpatrick's cavalry—some 5,000 strong—could deliver a decisive blow. But the enemy was not so easily outmaneuvered. The lack of cover and the resulting exposure to enemy fire left the West Virginians vulnerable, and the anticipated cavalry strike never came to pass.

However, Kilpatrick, ever hopeful, refused to abandon his vision.

Even in the face of failure, he saw a flicker of opportunity, clinging to the hope that the tide might turn in his favor. It was this same misguided optimism that led to the second charge, one that would prove to be even more disastrous than the first.

Kilpatrick, sensing a shift in the enemy's attention as Confederate Colonel Law's forces were diverted to the west, made the fateful decision to command Farnsworth's brigade to launch another charge. Farnsworth, in a move that defied all reason, led his men straight into their deaths.

Once his incompetence and evident disregard for his men's safety came into the spotlight, what little was left of his credibility was tarnished. And everything he did or said was up for debate. And that was when an already infuriated Henry Parsons found his window to bring forth the truth.

"Their assault was so bold that the Confederates received it as the advance of a grand attack, and, finding themselves exposed to infantry in front and cavalry in the rear, they were uncertain of their position. Why no advantage was taken of this, it is not for us to explain. Why the infantry, when they heard fighting in Law's rear, or when, afterward, we delivered to their skirmish line our prisoners, did not advance and drive his brigade into the valley where it would have been exposed to a general flank attack, has never been explained; but it was not 'a charge of madmen with a mad leader.' We believed, and yet believe, that Farnsworth's charge was wisely ordered, well-timed, well-executed, and effective."

He emphasized the accuracy of his account, noting:

"I have been carefully over the ground and have had the assistance of Colonel Batchelor and his guides in the preparation of the map that is appended."

More than a century later, renewed interest in the Farnsworth charge led to further scrutiny of that very map.

Andrea Custer, who was then engaged in writing a book on the Farnsworth charge, felt a growing unease with the prevailing interpretation of the charge's location. After years of studying the battle and conducting tours, she began to suspect inconsistencies in the accepted placement of key positions.

Custer was especially puzzled by how Parsons—despite his detailed account of the charge—had overlooked certain aspects of the terrain, and how his collaboration with Colonel Batchelor, Superintendent of Tablets and Legends, contributed to these inaccuracies. Flaws that had long gone uncorrected due to Batchelor's authoritative role in determining monument locations at Gettysburg National Military Park.

Her investigation yielded compelling evidence.

In the late 1890s, a group of New York veterans petitioned to have their state's monument relocated. They argued that Batchelor's decision had been erroneous and demonstrated that the New York monument should have stood half a mile southwest of its original placement. This misplacement also affected the positioning of the 1st Vermont and Pennsylvania monuments, which were subsequently erected in locations inconsistent with the true course of the battle.

While the New York monument was eventually moved to its rightful position, the Vermont and Pennsylvania markers were not. Custer located the base of the original New York monument and, using monument maps, determined that adjusting the positions of the remaining markers by the same southwestward distance aligned them with Parsons' original description of the charge. The confusion likely arose from the similar topography between the incorrect and correct sites.

It not only restored credibility to Colonel Parsons' account but also calls into question long-held assumptions about the geography of Farnsworth's charge—offering a more accurate framework for understanding one of Gettysburg's most debated cavalry actions and for giving recognition to those like Farnsworth, whose courage had been overshadowed by historical oversight.

It was in recalling them that Henry had once set down the following lines, a quiet benediction to the forgotten:

"No stone marks where he fell; no resolution of Congress or Legislature records his heroism. His commanding officer forgot his name. Yet we may not greatly wonder or complain, other heroes fell unnoticed, other brilliant movements were unmentioned. Where millions of men joined in a great war such was a necessity. What is written is a poor index of what may never be told. This compensation, however, comes. The brave men who were there, for conviction's sake, facing North and facing South, made the word 'American' a heroic term."

5

Through Thick and Thin

"Gettysburg Near the Battlefield July 4th 1863 My darling Nellie, The paralysis having nearly left my right arm, its first act after dropping the sword shall be to write you.

I am severely but not dangerously wounded. I led the third and deadly charge—Every one of us that reached the height was either killed or wounded.

Lieut. Watson's horse was shot. Capt. Cushman is, I fear, dead. He was at my side. We were separated, and I have neither seen nor heard from him since. He may be a prisoner, but I tremble.

It was a terrible strike: 400 Guides charged upon two brigades of infantry posted behind stone walls. Heaven only saved our lines. Had they fired lower just once, they might have emptied every saddle, but the bullets passed over us. Shots flew all around me; fifteen minutes later, at one point, a bullet was aimed straight at my heart, but I uttered a prayer and thought of the "armor" and rode through it. One placed his rifle at my side and fired. One bullet struck my rib and glanced off. One passed through my elbow, one wounded my horse, and I passed through that terrible fire otherwise unharmed.

I was taken prisoner on the 30th at the fight at Hanover, being very sick at that time and in an ambulance that was captured.

I hope I never write you again, Nellie, amid such horrible surroundings, and yet we are even cheerful here, for we feel that we have had a most unglorious past in the first conflict, which is resulting so gloriously to our aims."

Henry Parsons wrote to his beloved, Ellen Jane "Nellie" Loomis, as soon as his pain allowed him.

She needed to know he was alive. That was the point.

However, she also needed to hear his voice in those sentences, not the hollow echo of the man who'd led the third charge up the hill and walked back half-dead. So, he lightened his words where he could, folded in hope where there was only exhaustion. He told her he had prayed in the saddle and thought of armor, and in that moment, she had been there with him—though he never said so directly. She would understand.

His handwriting faltered midway through, a smudge where the pain took hold again. He pressed his lips together and finished the line anyway.

What he didn't write was that he feared who he might become after this. That something had shifted—not just in his arm, but in the marrow of him. He had looked down the barrel of death, and it had not blinked.

Henry had first met Nellie in 1863, when his cavalry company was stationed in Fairfax County, Virginia. The land near the Potomac still bore the traces of an earlier generation of Loomises.

Their initial meeting must have been brief, and yet something in that encounter had lingered with him through the fevered months of combat and convalescence. He had begun writing to her, perhaps tentatively at first, unsure of her reception, but soon with growing affection.

A sizable collection of those letters—earnest, often poetic, sometimes pleading—had survived. The bundle from the summer and fall of 1863 later held by Mrs. Robert Irvin of State College, Pennsylvania.

They spoke of a young cavalryman who, having survived the horror of Gettysburg, now waged a more personal campaign: that of convincing Nellie to be his wife.

Parsons first proposed marriage on August 9, 1863. It was a bold move for a man so recently wounded, both in body and spirit. Nellie's response, preserved in a letter to her brother George Loomis dated September 7, was disarmingly frank. She wrote of the moment with an almost clinical clarity:

"Several letters were written and received—I designed, of course, this should close the conflict forever—I told him plumply that the difference of age was an insurmountable objection— then, the little fact that I did not love him had some weight with me. I felt much as one does after sweeping the rubbish out."

Her words, while firm, were not cruel. She had drawn a boundary—decisively, she believed. And yet, the letters did not stop. Nor did the man. Time, war, and a certain quiet persistence would alter the course of their story.

Even as Henry pressed his case with Nellie, an avalanche of grief was quietly gathering behind him. Only two months after the carnage at Gettysburg left him wounded and reflective, another blow arrived. On September 1, 1863, his younger brother, John Hains Parsons, died in a Washington, D.C. hospital.

Like his brother, John had served in the 5th North Carolina Cavalry, and had only recently been promoted to quartermaster sergeant—a role of considerable responsibility within the regiment. His death, likely the result of one of the many virulent diseases that swept through Civil War encampments and hospitals, extinguished a life full of promise at just twenty-one.

The grief had scarcely begun to settle before more sorrow followed. Five months after John's passing, the Parsons family was again plunged into mourning when Henry's sister, Catherine, died at the age of nineteen. She had been battling the same debilitating condition that would later claim the life of Collette Loomis—rheumatoid arthritis, a disease poorly understood and nearly untreatable at the time.

In the midst of all the sadness that had enveloped the Parsons family—a season marked by loss, unanswered prayers, and the quiet, aching weight of absence—one event managed to pierce the gloom and offer Henry a measure of solace.

Nellie, gradually and perhaps to her own surprise, agreed to his long-standing proposal.

Despite initial reservations—she was six years his senior and had expressed concerns about their age difference—their bond deepened over time. Through the slow dance of ink and waiting,

Henry proved not only his constancy but the depth of his regard. And that was what won her over.

In one of his letters, dated October 1863, he finds himself particularly reflective. It is not simply a love letter, though love saturates every line. It is a document of emotional reckoning, a quiet confession of what it means to imagine a future after having nearly lost everything.

He writes:

"Shall I tell you how I feel? I can hardly tell how I feel, at times very sad, at times very cheerful. Just as one always feels when they see some great prize within reach and he yet is barred for a little time from grasping it—I feel very anxious for the time to come when the last wait shall be performed making us one in life and love—I feel to thank God for all those kind providences which brought and kept us together and give us common hopes, desires, sympathies, and plans; which gave us to each other—I feel glad, proud and thankful that such a woman has been led to love, trust, and confide her heart and hand to my keeping—I feel solemnly impressed with responsibilities I assume in accepting the charge of so much trust and good—I feel a new ambition and a high resolve to prove myself worthy of Nellie and to make her love me wholly influencing my every thought and giving a new tone to my feelings."

They got married on New Year's Eve, their vows whispered as sleet ticked against the windows, while somewhere beyond the frost-rimed glass, the war ground on without them.

After their wedding, Henry and Nellie's lives unfolded across the alternating geography of St. Albans and West Springfield—two towns, two worlds, neither of which could contain all that they had lived through. Henry could not entirely shed the soldier he had been.

His body had returned, but his mind would sometimes travel back to the sounds of cannons, to the weight of muskets on his shoulder, to the faces of men whose names had long since faded from memory but whose lives he still carried with him.

The healing he sought was not simply of the body, but of the mind, and in St. Albans, he found a place to begin that work—*but only just.*

By spring, when the thaw of winter turned the landscape into a canvas of fresh possibilities, they would leave St. Albans behind, at least for a while. They would make the journey south to West Springfield, a town that had been a cradle for Henry's pre-war dreams.

Here, amid the bustle of a more active life, Henry felt the pulse of his old ambitions. In this place, he was not just a man recovering from the trauma of war; he was a man seeking to return to the life he had once envisioned for himself before his service in the Union Army.

However, every step he took was a reminder that the past could not be outrun. The familiarity of the town did not offer him the clean slate he had hoped for. There was, instead, a quiet dissonance between who he was now and the man he had once believed himself to be.

And then there was the guilt. The constant, gnawing sense that he could have done more. That he might have saved one more man, stood firmer in the chaos of retreat, shouted a clearer order when confusion reigned.

The war was over, but its *unfinished* conversations clung to him like smoke.

He never spoke these thoughts aloud. To do so would have felt indulgent, even shameful. After all, he had come home. He had a wife who loved him, a home that held him, and the whisper of a future trying to bloom.

Yet, gratitude could not outpace the sense that something had been taken unfairly from others and unfairly given to him. He had stood too many times beside lifeless bodies, had written too many names in small ledgers, had helped dig too many shallow graves. The arithmetic of survival made no sense.

And so, when the evenings grew long and the town quieted into its own kind of slumber, Henry would sometimes find himself staring out the window at nothing in particular.

The glass pane offered little reflection—only the faintest ghost of his own face in the lamplight, hollow-eyed and still. Beyond it, the world lay in silence: rooftops sunk in shadow, chimney smoke curling indifferently into the dusk, the occasional clatter of hooves down Main Street growing rarer as night took hold. But all Henry saw was a war that still raged on in the sodden fields of the South and the weary camps holding the line.

And he wanted—*achingly*, almost irrationally—to return to it.

He could not stomach the comfort of a chair by the fire while others marched barefoot in the snow. He felt, in some secret chamber of his heart, that he had not finished what he was meant to do. That by surviving, he had incurred a kind of debt—a moral obligation to give more than he already had. But he couldn't.

The discharge paper, signed and final, sat folded in a drawer like a verdict. His body, battered and unreliable, had made the decision for him. And so, he sat.

Torn between the duties of the present and the unresolved mission of the past. Between Nellie's warm presence and the cold memory of men who had no such home to return to. The guilt of surviving was now paired with the agony of helplessness. He was a soldier without a war, a witness with no power to intervene.

He didn't let Nellie catch a wind of what was going on inside him. He didn't want to invite her into a place she didn't deserve to go. He told himself he was protecting her. Shielding her from the weight he carried. The night terrors. The quiet grief that settled over him without warning.

He kept it hidden behind polite smiles, behind long walks he took alone, behind the pause before answering when she asked how he was. He swallowed it with his coffee, folded it away with his uniform, tucked it into the corners of his silence. But Nellie knew. She always knew.

However, she never pressed. That wasn't her way. But she made room for his silences. She met his distance not with complaint, but with the quiet assurance of her presence. If he drifted, she anchored. If he brooded, she busied herself nearby, letting the scent of supper or the rustle of her mending speak the kind of comfort words could not.

'For better or for worse.' Nellie stood by her vows.

She had fallen in love with a man who was headed to war—full of conviction and unweathered resolve—but the man who returned was still mid-crossing. And so, she loved both versions: the boy she had once known, and the man who sometimes couldn't find his way fully back to her. For beneath all the layers of hurt and distortions, he was still the Henry she once knew. And she wasn't about to give up on that.

6

Steel Ambitions

With the passage of time, a subtle metamorphosis took place within Henry, imperceptible at first, but unmistakable in its quiet progression. The visceral weight of his war-ravaged soul, while never entirely exorcised, began to loosen its stranglehold. And in its absence, his ambition returned. For the first time in many months, Henry felt the stirrings of focus, of the quiet drive that once propelled him toward the future.

In the study of law, Henry began to see the world through a transformed lens, one shaped not by the blunt force of battle but by the more refined tools of reason, logic, and precedent. The field, with its intricate frameworks and weighty principles, invited him to look beyond the immediate, urging him to consider not only the letter of the rules but their deeper implications—the subtle interplay between justice and equity, between authority and conscience.

It was a world where nuance reigned and where every assertion, every action, required careful scrutiny, where facts were not merely accepted but interrogated, where the most complex truths often lay hidden beneath the surface. It was where he regained some of his agency and discovered within himself a newfound purpose.

This awakening was paired with a growing confidence in his own judgment. What had once been instinct honed on the battlefield matured into something sharper: *discernment.* He possessed a newly fortified self-assurance—an ability to assess risk not just with the caution of a survivor, but with the seasoned clarity of one who had witnessed, firsthand, the cost of poor leadership and shortsighted decisions.

Intent on forging a future unmarred by the shadows of war, Henry resettled his young family in Richmond—a city still veiled in the residue of its fallen grandeur, where brick facades bore the scorches of surrender and ambition lingered like dust in the rafters. It was there that he undertook the bar examination and was duly admitted to the Virginia bar.

But Henry's vision extended far beyond the courtroom. Like many farsighted men of his generation, he saw that the future belonged to steel and steam—to the spines of iron that would bind the fractured nation and carry it forward.

Financial prosperity, he believed, lay in the development of existing railroads, the construction of new lines, and the strategic mining of coal and iron to feed the engines of industry.

This was not mere speculation—it was a conviction rooted in observation, shaped by a mind attuned to patterns of growth and the interdependence of law, commerce, and geography. In the veins of the railroad and the dark seams of Appalachian coal, Henry saw not just profit, but progress. He believed that through them, a wounded country could find its footing once more—and that he, in his modest but resolute way, could help lay the tracks.

And so, Henry made his move.

He began by positioning himself as the attorney for Putnam County, West Virginia, a role that would allow him to gain a foothold in the region's legal and political circles. It was not merely a position of convenience—it was a strategic entry into a world of influence.

The county's legal affairs provided him with valuable insight into the intersections of law, land, and commerce in the region. He understood that the real power lay in the connections he could make within them. He cultivated these ties with the precision of a man who knew that, in a fractured country, the true currency was influence.

For the next two years, Henry methodically gathered information. He learned the intimate details of the railroad industry, from the precarious financial standing of key players to the long-term visions that some men had for the country's infrastructure. More importantly, he identified the men whose decisions could shape that future—and he made it a point to be seen, to be noticed, by them.

One such man was William C. Wickham, a figure whose reputation, both in the South and beyond, was as complicated as it was influential.

Wickham, a former Confederate brigadier general, had turned the page of history with unexpected audacity—choosing to ally himself with the Republican cause after the war, a move that had attracted both admiration and suspicion.

As the principal holder of the Chesapeake and Ohio Railroad Company, Wickham held considerable sway over the future of the railroad industry in the region. His importance was not lost on Henry, who recognized that forming a friendship with this man could open doors to influence far beyond what his current position might provide.

Over time, Henry and Wickham became acquainted, their conversations shifting from polite pleasantries to discussions of business, land, and the inevitable future of railroads.

Wickham spoke not merely of trains and timetables, but of arteries of commerce that would reconnect the Eastern seaboard to the mineral-rich backbone of the Appalachians. At the heart of his endeavor was the revitalization and unification of three separate rail lines—each a fragment of antebellum ambition now languishing in postwar disrepair.

The Virginia Central Railroad, first chartered in 1836 under the name Louisa Railroad, began as a modest enterprise intended to link the agricultural heartlands of central Virginia with the state capital. But over time, its ambitions grew—and with them, its name. By the mid-1850s, rechristened as the Virginia Central, the line had become the keystone in a bold vision: to transform Richmond, still reeling from the loss of its tobacco monopoly, into a vital entrepôt for inland commerce.

The rails pushed westward with stubborn resolve, carving through rolling piedmonts and into the Blue Ridge, until at last they reached Covington—perilously close to the Ohio River but halted at the base of the Alleghenies.

There, the iron tide ebbed.

The coming of war froze all forward movement; Union raids and Confederate requisitioning crippled the line. Bridges were razed, tracks were torn from their beds and melted into cannonballs, and depots were reduced to ash. What had once been the pride of Virginia's internal improvement campaign now lay in twisted ruin, a casualty of both ambition and artillery.

To this battered spine, Wickham fused the Blue Ridge Railroad—a state-funded undertaking conceived to conquer the natural barrier that had checked Virginia Central's advance: the mountains themselves. Chartered by the Commonwealth in 1849 and entrusted to the formidable mind of Claudius Crozet, a French-born military engineer who had once taught at West Point, the Blue Ridge had been conceived to tunnel through stone, linking the Virginia Central's eastern momentum to the untapped lands beyond.

Crozet's vision culminated in the Blue Ridge Tunnel, a four-thousand-foot bore drilled by hand through dense granite beneath Rockfish Gap. The work was punishing and perilous, relying heavily on the labor of recently arrived Irish immigrants and hundreds of enslaved African Americans conscripted by the state. Death was frequent, progress was slow, and the technical challenges were monumental. Yet by 1858, the tunnel stood as the longest of its kind in the Western Hemisphere—a subterranean triumph heralded in engineering journals and newspaper columns alike.

However, war, as it had with the Virginia Central, brought decay.

The third, and perhaps most daunting, of Wickham's ambitions was the Covington and Ohio—a railroad that, for all its promise, had existed largely in the realm of theory. Conceived in 1853 with the hope of extending Virginia's rail network through the Allegheny Mountains and onto the Ohio River, this line was a grand prospect that remained nothing more than a blueprint.

The work was consistently stymied by the difficult terrain and even more by the lack of capital and political support. Then, the outbreak of war in 1861 sealed its fate. The same Union raids that ravaged the Virginia Central, the same Confederate requisitions that stripped the Commonwealth of vital resources, left the Atlantic, Mississippi, and Ohio in tatters.

Wickham, however, was not deterred by the ghosts of failed plans. He was not yet ready to forsake his vision for the Chesapeake and Ohio Railway—*C&O*, as he called the unified network of the three lines. If anything, the desolation left in war's wake deepened his resolve.

In an era when speculative ventures abounded and every city council and prairie township clamored for funding, Wickham ventured a bold appeal: an offering of ten million dollars in thirty-year bonds bearing seven percent interest. It was a handsome yield, calculated to attract both domestic financiers and European syndicates still wary after America's internecine collapse.

To demonstrate that his ambitions were grounded in more than parchment and rhetoric, Wickham authorized a critical stretch of construction—from Covington to the mineral springs of White Sulphur in West Virginia.

The undertaking, though modest in mileage, cut through some of the most recalcitrant terrain east of the Mississippi. Workers wrestled with granite outcrops, swollen creeks, and unstable cuts, laying track with pick and shovel while mountain storms soaked the earth to slurry. Camps rose along the right-of-way—clusters of tents and timber bunkhouses where the air reeked of sweat, coal smoke, and boiled salt pork.

Progress was hard-won, but visible. Wickham wagered that these tangible gains—rails driven, ties tamped, locomotives steaming under their own power—would draw investors the way iron draws the compass. But the financial markets did not oblige.

The year 1869 brought no gold rush of bond sales. Despite Wickham's tireless promotion, despite the engineering feats already in hand, the C&O's bond issue foundered. The appetite for long-term infrastructure debt was already dulled by a glut of similar offerings, and the C&O—obscure, half-built, scarred by the legacy of Confederate collapse—was passed over in favor of shinier prospects.

Bankers in New York hesitated. Agents in London demurred. The South's economic repute, still mired in Reconstruction stigma, did the railroad no favors.

By winter's end, only a trickle of subscriptions had been received, and the company faced a staggering burden: over one million dollars in debt for a line that still had not crested the Alleghenies.

Wickham received the news with outward stoicism, but those close to him noted a change. The letters came more slowly. The speeches grew graver. His famously clipped diction—once sharp with conviction—began to bear the weight of calculation, of contingency. He was a man whose dreams had reached the anvil of circumstance, and now found the hammer falling hard.

Henry saw that the path ahead would require more than faith. It would require *daring*.

With a sense of desperation sharpened by duty, he took the burden upon himself. He had long possessed a gift for persuasion, but now he would stake his reputation—and what remained of the C&O's future—on one final bid for salvation. Through business connections and sheer determination, he managed to secure the attention of two influential financiers: Harvey Fisk and Alfrederick Hatch. Titans of Wall Street with ties to transcontinental ventures, the men were skeptical, yet intrigued.

That was more than enough.

Fisk and Hatch listened, but demurred. They were not prepared to underwrite the venture themselves. Yet, perhaps recognizing Henry's clarity—or perhaps moved by his sheer refusal to yield—they agreed to arrange an introduction to someone who might: Collis P. Huntington.

One of the so-called "Big Four" of the Central Pacific Railroad, Huntington had grown rich off the completion of the transcontinental line and had begun turning his attention eastward. He was shrewd, calculating, and unencumbered by regional loyalties. If the C&O stood any chance in the market, it could only be possible if Huntington saw the opportunity for what it was: a way to extend his growing empire into the South's postwar landscape.

However, Huntington was no philanthropist. He needed quite a bit of convincing. Between C&O's evident financial difficulties and his reputation for dismissals, Fisk and Hatch were the only two people who could make that possible. Huntington owed them.

Though he would one day be enshrined by journalists and financiers as "the leading railroad builder of the United States," in the spring of 1869, Collis Huntington was not a man ascending. He was a man exhausted—bruised by political and personal battles, and clinging to his empire by a fraying thread of leverage.

The Pacific Railroad had, by then, reached its terminus at Promontory Summit, where the golden spike was driven with great fanfare. It was a moment for the history books, for engravings and oratory, for the smug applause of railroad barons and government men. But Huntington had not been present for the photo-op.

Though his name was etched into the financial and operational backbone of the Central Pacific, he was notably absent from the jubilant ceremony. Whether by omission or intent, the Eastern press had largely overlooked him.

Behind the scenes, the completion of the line had drained him—financially and emotionally. The Central Pacific, once a wellspring of cash and Congressional goodwill, had become a weight around his neck. The company owed $1.25 million to Philip Speyer & Company, the American outpost of a powerful Frankfurt brokerage.

Worse still, Huntington faced semiannual interest payments nearing twenty million dollars on bonds issued in flurries during the frenzied years of track-laying. His auxiliary firm—the rather opaquely named Contract & Finance Company—was also tethered to a staggering $3.5 million in floating debt, much of it anchored by personal guarantees from five associates, whose faith in the endeavor was starting to tremble. Interest alone consumed twelve to fifteen percent, a cruel math that made every passing week more precarious.

Psychologically, too, Huntington was depleted. He had spent years wrangling not just Congress but a rogues' gallery of fellow railroad men—dreamers, schemers, and armchair visionaries who alternately sought his favor and questioned his tactics. Many had tested his patience, some had betrayed his trust, and a few had earned his contempt. Huntington had endured, but not without scars.

So, when Fisk and Hatch came to him—not as supplicants, but as allies who had once carried water for his cause—he listened. Their firm helped him unload tens of millions in Central Pacific and government bonds, often snapping up the securities themselves to hold the price aloft when the market turned cold. They had stood by him when others fled. Therefore, Huntington, for all his brusqueness, was not without a memory for loyalty. It was now time to return the favor. That's when the meeting was set up.

In the waning days of spring 1869, Henry Parsons arrived at 17 William Street in New York City, a modest building in the financial quarter where Collis P. Huntington kept his operations. The air outside pulsed with the grind of dray carts, the murmur of clerks, and the distant clatter of hooves echoing off the granite façades. Inside, the corridors smelled of coal smoke and ink, and the business of empire was conducted in tones just above a whisper.

Henry came prepared not with a plea, but with a presentation—an engineer's bundle of blueprints, elevation diagrams, and meticulously drawn gradients, unfolded like battle maps across Huntington's desk.

Among them, folded with care and placed near the top, was a letter dated September 21, 1868, bearing the unmistakable signature of General Robert E. Lee. In it, Lee had endorsed the potential of the Chesapeake and Ohio Railway with solemn precision: the C&O, he wrote, "will furnish the most advantageous route from the Mississippi Valley to the Atlantic," and "may become one of the principal eastern branches of the Pacific Railroad." For Henry, whose lineage traced back through Virginia soil and sorrow, Lee's imprimatur was not simply symbolic—it was strategic currency.

Huntington did not so much as glance at it.

He sat motionless, sphinx-like, beneath a portrait of President Lincoln rendered in stippled charcoal. His fingers were templed beneath his chin; his gaze, fixed on Henry, was unreadable. He asked no questions. He offered no interruptions. He gave no indication that he had even heard. It was not disdain—not overtly—but something colder: indifference polished to the level of art.

Henry spoke with measured clarity, outlining the economic logic of the line, its untapped mineral corridor through the Alleghenies, its strategic tie to the eastward sweep of the national trade routes. He invoked not nostalgia, but inevitability: the South would rise, not in rebellion, but in rails. Still, Huntington remained opaque, his silence echoing in the wooden floorboards like a rebuke.

At length, Parsons rolled up the last of his charts and gathered his papers with a practiced efficiency that barely concealed the blow. He had entered the room bearing the embers of a grand vision. He left it scorched by a silence he could not decipher.

Outside, the city resumed its mechanical hum—paperboys cried headlines, steam whistles blared from the harbor, and the future marched on without hesitation. Parsons descended the stoop and stepped into the clamor, convinced, in that moment, that he had failed—that the Chesapeake and Ohio had breathed its last before a man who could resurrect it with a single nod and chose, instead, to say nothing at all.

However, back in the corridors of Wall Street, Fisk and Hatch did not share his gloom. Seasoned brokers and veterans of industrial persuasion, they had seen the look in Huntington's eyes before—not of dismissal, but of calculation. Henry had presented more than a failing railroad; he had delivered, unwittingly, a puzzle worth solving. And Huntington, for all his silence, was a man who detested loose ends.

Their instincts would prove sound.

On June 9, 1869, scarcely a week after Henry's presentation, a document arrived from Huntington's office, penned in his unmistakable script. Unadorned, businesslike, and precise, it bore the full weight of his decision—a proposal that, if accepted, would alter the trajectory of the Chesapeake & Ohio Railway and breathe life into its flagging ambitions.

The terms were stark and clear. The C&O was to rescind its recent issuance of ten million dollars in seven-percent thirty-year bonds, an offering which had languished without takers and tethered the company to mounting liabilities. In its place, the company would issue fifteen million dollars in six-percent bonds—more favorable, more palatable to the increasingly cautious investment houses of New York and London.

Of this new offering, Huntington's syndicate would purchase the first million—an initial stake designed to restore credibility and signal institutional confidence. But the financial infusion was only the beginning.

In exchange, Huntington's consortium would secure controlling interest in the company's common stock—eight million dollars' worth—delivered in four installments as the rails advanced across the rugged terrain of West Virginia. This was no mere patronage; it was a calculated assumption of power. The syndicate would not simply underwrite the railroad—they would shape it, govern it, and ultimately claim its destiny as their own.

Huntington himself pledged no idle fortune. Rather, he offered his name, his acumen, and the formidable machinery of his financial apparatus. His syndicate, forged from the cadre of men who had driven spikes through deserts and mountains alike, would fully leverage their engineering prowess, political influence, and operational discipline.

The terms laid forth were, by any measure, severe.

They stripped the Chesapeake & Ohio of its autonomy and placed its destiny squarely in the hands of a man whose allegiance was to enterprise, not geography. Yet in the autumn of 1869, with credit in tatters and hope dwindling by the day, Henry Parsons and the leadership of the C&O found themselves with little room to maneuver. The railroad's options had narrowed to a *single corridor*—and Huntington held the key.

In late summer, a meeting was convened at White Sulphur Springs, the storied mountain resort in Greenbrier County, where steam-heated parlors and mineral-rich baths could not soothe the urgency of the deliberations underway. There, President Williams C. Wickham, along with the railroad's board of directors, gathered across from Huntington, who remained cool, self-possessed, and, above all, immovable.

He had come to negotiate, but not to compromise.

His terms were laid out with the precision of a surveyor's chain: There would be no partial terms, no shared authority. He would inject capital only if granted effective ownership. Wickham and the others—*men of honor but not of capital*—had no real leverage. With little ceremony, they yielded.

The C&O passed into new hands.

7

Metamorphosis

While the ink dried on the papers that ceded the Chesapeake & Ohio to Collis Huntington, a different kind of crisis was rippling through the corridors of American finance.

Just weeks after the gentlemen adjourned from White Sulphur Springs, the country was rocked by the spectacle of *Black Friday*—September 24, 1869—when the price of gold surged to dangerous heights and then collapsed with equal violence.

The panic had been engineered with brazen cunning.

Jay Gould and James Fisk, already infamous for their exploits at the Erie Railroad, had sought to corner the gold market through a network of political influence, speculative buying, and public manipulation. With the tacit complicity of officials close to the Grant administration, they sent the price of gold soaring, prompting hoarding, export freezes, and general monetary paralysis.

When the federal government finally intervened—ordering the sale of $4 million in gold to break the corner—the market turned on its axis. In a matter of hours, prices collapsed, credit contracted, and a wave of financial wreckage radiated outward from Wall Street.

To many, it was a calamity. But to Huntington, it was confirmation.

He had long distrusted the ephemeral glitter of speculation, preferring the slow, architectural work of infrastructure—steel, timber, land, and time. The crash underscored what he already believed: that fortunes built on paper could vanish in an afternoon, but a railroad, once laid, could shape nations.

More to the point, it sharpened his resolve to wrest the C&O from the domain of regional sentiment and into the sphere of national consequence. With capital markets rattled and investors skittish, the Virginians could not hope to compete. The $850,000 Huntington had managed to raise—short of his promised million but solid in a time of doubt—now seemed a gift from higher ground. On November 15, with little debate, Wickham and the stockholders accepted it in full satisfaction of his terms.

Now president of the line, with Wickham retained as vice president and general superintendent, Huntington set about transforming the railroad from a Southern relic into a trans-regional artery. The C&O would no longer be tethered to war-haunted memories or local boosterism. It would be an east-west corridor of commerce, drawn with the precision of empire and backed by the solidity of his syndicate's capital.

And in Henry Parsons, newly named company director and general agent for the territory west of the Alleghenies, Huntington retained a crucial bridge to the vision's origins—one that would soon prove vital as the line pushed toward the Ohio River and beyond.

But first, there was the matter of finding a terminus.

The site needed to satisfy a trinity of demands: proximity to navigable waters, access to abundant land at minimal cost, and the capacity to support the industrial infrastructure of a modern rail depot. After careful evaluation, attention settled on a tract of wilderness at the confluence of the Guyandotte River and the Ohio—a landscape of muddy banks, timbered slopes, and untapped promise.

Here, Huntington quietly secured some five thousand acres of land—an acquisition notable not only for its scale but for the speed and discretion with which it was executed. To formalize the venture and manage its development, he organized the Central Land Company, an enterprise as deliberately constructed as any of his rail concerns.

The goal was not simply to purchase land, but to impose a *vision* upon it.

On February 27, 1871, the new town was officially incorporated under the name Huntington, WV—an act that merged self-interest with posterity.

Within the town's nascent boundaries rose the essential fixtures of a railroad city: expansive shops for locomotive repair and construction, two orderly rows of workers' dwellings constructed for lease to the men who would soon arrive by the dozens and then hundreds, and a rudimentary civic grid drawn not by custom, but by business.

It was in this critical moment that Henry Parsons took up the mantle.

As the railroad's trusted agent west of the Alleghenies, he took responsibility not merely for the tracks that sliced through rugged terrain, but for *nurturing* the human element that would sustain the enterprise. When he and his wife Nellie relocated to the town of Huntington, WV, in 1870 with their daughters Kate and Grace, they became among the first families to plant roots in what was still, in many ways, a frontier settlement.

There, at 725 Ninth Street, Henry oversaw the construction of a gracious two-story white-frame house—an edifice not merely of timber and paint, but of intention, aspiration, and deep personal investment.

The structure rose with a quiet dignity from the red earth of the fledgling town, its broad front porch adorned with slender turned columns, inviting respite and reflection in the soft shade of a West Virginia summer. Tall, double-hung sash windows offered symmetry and sunlight in equal measure, while a central gable added a note of architectural pride. Inside, the home featured high ceilings, plaster walls, and polished hardwood floors—each detail chosen not for opulence but for endurance.

Each room held a trove of memories: the heavy oak dining table around which the family gathered, the modest parlors where lessons were learned and stories shared, and the hearth that warmed countless winter evenings with flickering light and the scent of woodsmoke.

Within this haven, Kate, Grace, and later Maud cultivated their earliest understandings of the world—shaped not only by parental guidance but by the subtle lessons of resilience, hope, and rootedness imparted by the very structure that sheltered them. The house was more than mere shelter; it was a repository of *identity*, a canvas upon which the delicate brushstrokes of youth were painted—moments of innocence, burgeoning curiosity, and the gradual unfolding of ambition.

By the opening days of January 1873, the contours of a once-aspirational vision—one to which Henry had lent his labor, judgment, and unshakable belief—had at last cohered into tangible form. The final length of the Chesapeake & Ohio Railroad was laid and made ready.

On the crisp morning of January 22, as frost clung to eaves and the scent of coal smoke mingled with winter air, the whistle of a locomotive pierced the quiet—heralding not only the culmination of a great engineering feat, but also the arrival of the man whose *determination* had helped make it possible.

For Henry, that moment was freighted with emotion: a convergence of duty fulfilled and hope realized, as the landscape he had once surveyed as wilderness now bore the unmistakable marks of progress.

With the rails now binding the Atlantic tidewater to the western edge of Virginia, focus shifted from mere connection to cultivation—of industry, of infrastructure, and of the vast natural resources that lay waiting beyond the horizon. Coal seams, timber stands, and mineral veins—once remote and economically inert—were suddenly within reach, and Huntington stood poised as both depot and gateway.

Henry was not one to rest in the wake of achievement.

By 1879, his ambitions extended eastward toward a corridor of opportunity that had long languished in disuse: the James River and Kanawha Canal. Once imagined as a waterborne bridge between Richmond and the Ohio Valley, the canal had slipped into obsolescence—its stonework crumbling, its waters stilled. Yet he saw in its disuse a kind of advantage. The terrain had already been surveyed, the route carved, the elevation tamed. All it lacked was a new purpose.

Seizing the moment, he aligned with a syndicate of industrialists—among them Cyrus McCormick—to acquire the canal property and establish the Richmond and Alleghany Railroad. The venture was bold in both scale and structure. To bind their intent with irrevocable purpose, the group deposited a forfeit of $500,000—a guarantee that the line would be completed within fourteen months. It was not a speculative gesture, but a calculated bet on disciplined engineering and relentless logistics.

Under Henry's exacting supervision, the enterprise advanced with relentless momentum. Trestles were thrown across swift tributaries, passageways were blasted through escarpments, and the towpath—long since surrendered to vine and weather—was reborn as a dynamic conduit of commerce. Construction teams moved with mechanical precision, hewing progress from stone and soil with the same determination that had driven the rails west.

The undertaking met its deadline.

On time, under pressure, and without compromise, the Richmond and Alleghany line opened—a testament to what could be achieved when vision, capital, and leadership converged.

No longer confined to fieldwork or logistical oversight, Henry transitioned into the executive arena with a portfolio that quickly diversified. Appointed vice president of the Richmond & Alleghany Railroad, he stepped into a strategic role, guiding the line's operations through a critical period of integration and expansion.

Yet railroads alone did not define his growing sphere of influence.

He went on to serve as president of the Alleghany Coal and Iron Company, a dual-purpose enterprise that sought to harness the region's untapped mineral wealth and funnel it into national markets via the very railways he had helped to construct. These were not passive appointments; Henry held major financial stakes and directed company policy with a characteristic eye for scalability and return.

He soon expanded his reach to include executive leadership in the Atlantic and Northwestern Railway and the Kanawha Construction Company, the latter of which he led as both president and principal shareholder. Through these positions, Parsons became a linchpin in the evolving industrial matrix of the postwar South—a man as fluent in geology and supply chains as he was in surveyor's plots and financial ledgers.

Yet for all his triumphs in steel and stone, the work had extracted a private toll—one preserved only in the quiet archive of his wife's hand. While Henry rose through the ranks of postwar industry, Nellie remained at home, raising their daughters and writing letters that oscillated between pride and longing. She often inquired after his constitution, aware that his schedule, particularly during the final push to complete the Richmond and Alleghany line, had worn on his health.

The rigors of that fourteen-month gauntlet had left Henry diminished, his sleep shortened, his appetite erratic.

However, railways are not built by sentiment, and he did what the work demanded—pushed through fever, through fatigue, through the creeping sense that he was becoming a ghost in his own life. The line opened on time. The investors cheered. But when Henry stood at the inaugural ceremony, brass watch in hand, he could barely feel the weight of victory.

So, he *envisioned* something different.

With the most grueling years of construction behind him and his place in the industrial establishment secure, Henry began to contemplate a new kind of enterprise—one where residence and business might occupy the same parcel of land, enabling him to remain not only at the center of operations, but within reach of his family's daily life.

It was a shrewd move, yes—but also profoundly human. Years spent tracing rails westward, sleeping in drafty depots and eating by lantern light beside stone embankments had taught him that stillness could be as vital as motion. Here, at last, was a corner of the world not to be conquered, but tended—a hearth rather than a horizon.

8

The Measure of Belonging

The Natural Bridge of Rockbridge County was no idle vanity. Though undeniably picturesque, its value—at least to Henry Parsons—rested not in its grandeur, but in its untapped possibility. He was never one to chase landmarks for sentiment alone. Yet, in the waning chapter of his career, as the clang of hammers and hiss of steam slowly gave way to quieter ambitions, Parsons found himself drawn to this underappreciated limestone arch.

Nearly a century prior, amid the colonial administration of Virginia and the Crown's allotment of western lands, Thomas Jefferson had felt the same.

Back in 1774, Jefferson had paid twenty shillings for the Natural Bridge and 157 acres surrounding it, securing the parcel from King George III's land office with what he later called *"the most sublime of nature's works."*

In his early visits, long before rail lines threaded the Shenandoah Valley, Jefferson lodged where he could—

sometimes with friends nearby, at other times in the brick-built Hugh Barclay Tavern, which still stood in Parsons's day two miles upstream along Cedar Creek. Another favored stop was the more imposing Natural Bridge Tavern, a stone house near the Barclay property and by the 1880s the residence of Mrs. Wilson Whitmore.

Later, sometime after his presidency—perhaps as early as 1814—Jefferson constructed a small log retreat close to the crown of the arch. Though the original structure had vanished, its stone foundation remained, incorporated into what became known as the Jefferson Cottage: a modest frame dwelling along the ridge. For travellers approaching from the south along what would become Route 11, it was the first house passed on the left—a simple structure, yet steeped in provenance.

For decades, the property passed quietly through time, noted in journals and admired in engravings, but largely untouched. Jefferson never sold it. Even in his final years, as debts mounted and Monticello strained under the weight of financial gravity, the Natural Bridge remained in his portfolio— a rare constant in a life of turbulence.

When he died in 1826, the bridge was retained by his heirs, folded into the complex web of assets left to settle an unforgiving estate. Visitors continued to arrive, drawn not only by the spectacle itself but by the gravity of Jefferson's authorship. To stand beneath the arch was, for many, to touch the republic's early breath.

Through the ensuing decades, the property shifted hands— discreetly at first, and then with more evident design.

During the post-Civil War period, the ownership of the Natural Bridge transitioned into the hands of the Harman family, notably Michael Garber Harman—a Confederate officer in the 52nd Virginia Infantry and a well-known businessman who operated a stage line and hotel in Staunton. Harman had acquired the land shortly after the war, when many Southern properties changed ownership under economic duress. His acquisition marked the site's passage from hallowed inheritance into the realm of speculative enterprise.

As the century advanced and America's appetite for leisure widened, the Bridge began to emerge as an asset with potential yield. Pathways were cleared, railroads encroached, and the first stirrings of tourist infrastructure took root. Where once Jefferson had walked in philosophical solitude, others now arrived in pursuit of scenery, science, sentiment, or all three.

By the late 1870s, however, Harman's hold on the property had weakened. Though he had once prospered as a hotelier and transportation man, the postwar years brought steep financial headwinds. In 1880, litigation with the Valley National Bank of Staunton culminated in a court-ordered sale. A commissioner was appointed. The land, including the Natural Bridge and several hundred surrounding acres, would pass once more.

That's when Henry Parsons stepped forward.

The bid—$1,400—was modest. However, what it set in motion was anything but. Henry was no stranger to enterprise or expansion but here, the motive seemed quieter.

He saw in the Natural Bridge a locus of enduring value, where beauty could serve both spirit and livelihood. He envisioned travellers not merely pausing in awe, but remaining—lodging in newly built cottages, strolling curated paths, picnicking beneath old-growth pines, contributing to a regional economy increasingly driven by tourism and natural heritage.

And beneath that foresight stirred something more personal. For all his undertakings—from his wartime service to his legal and corporate posts—this may have been the first place he claimed not for advancement, but for meaning. Perhaps that was the deeper impulse: to mark a life not solely by what he had built or acquired, but by what he had chosen to *keep*.

At the heart of his vision stood the Forest Inn, a stately hotel erected atop the ridge overlooking the arch. Constructed in the picturesque style favored by the Gilded Age elite, the inn offered expansive verandas, soaring ceilings, and a commanding view of the surrounding Blue Ridge.

Around it, Henry curated an immersive resort landscape. He commissioned the construction of guest cottages and private cabins discreetly tucked into wooded clearings; a grand ballroom for evening assemblies; the Appledore Lodge—rustic yet elegantly appointed—nestled amid laurel groves; and a substantial gatehouse that served as both entrance and herald to the estate.

Supporting these were stables, a general store, service quarters, and a dedicated water and sewer system—remarkable infrastructural undertakings for the period and setting.

The grounds themselves were no less considered. Bridle paths wound through dappled glades, carriage roads traced the natural contours of the land, and promenades descended toward the base of the arch and the murmuring flow of Cedar Creek.

Yet Henry's most theatrical innovation came with nightfall: the Bridge was illuminated by a kaleidoscope of colored lanterns, gas-fed reflectors, and magnesium flares, transforming the natural span into a sublime spectacle of light and shadow—an effect few Americans had seen applied to the wilderness.

Situated roughly two miles from the nearest rail station, the place might have remained a remote curiosity were it not for his strategic initiative to astutely leverage the Richmond-Alleghany Railroad to expand access.

Henry had arranged for special excursion trains—seasonal and often scheduled on weekends or holidays—that ferried hundreds of visitors from Richmond, Lynchburg, and beyond to the scenic gateway of Rockbridge County. These were carefully orchestrated events, promising a curated experience of natural wonder paired with social refinement.

For many, the visit was a day-long affair: a guided tour of the Bridge itself, an elegant luncheon or dinner served at the Forest Inn or the stone tavern, and time spent exploring the grounds before the return journey. Yet a significant number of vacationers also lingered for weeks or the entire summer season, drawn by the fresh mountain air, the genteel hospitality, and the promise of respite from the bustle of city life.

As the resort flourished in popularity, it became a vital source of employment for the surrounding communities, offering livelihoods to a diverse array of local residents. Laborers found work maintaining the grounds, staffing the hotel and outbuildings, while area farmers supplied the establishment with essential provisions—fresh produce, dairy, and meats for the kitchen, alongside hay and feed to sustain the horses and other livestock integral to daily operations.

This interconnected venture invigorated several aspects of the regional economy: the railroads saw a rise in passenger numbers, locals enjoyed steady income, and Henry's resort continued to thrive as a prominent destination for recreation.

In response, and with an eye toward permanence, he and Nellie executed a significant legal transfer in 1884. They transferred ownership of the entire Natural Bridge property—including the resort complex, the Bridge itself, and the surrounding acreage—to the newly incorporated Natural Bridge Forest Company. By placing the property into a company structure, the Parsons sought to ensure continuity of stewardship, potential expansion of investment, and a means of managing the park's multiple moving parts within a more durable legal framework.

The structure proved effective.

By 1890, a deed transfer from the Forest Company to the more recent Natural Bridge Park Company placed operational focus specifically on the park's tourist-facing components—most notably, the Bridge and gatehouse. The move underscored the property's dual nature as both natural sanctuary and commercial enterprise. It has since been asserted that under this structure, Henry oversaw the largest privately owned park in the United States—a rare combination of civic spirit, entrepreneurial drive, and enduring affection for a place that had, in every sense, become his life's monument.

Yet this consolidation of property and purpose did not proceed without friction.

While Henry was becoming a celebrated figure in regional development, other members of the Parsons family—long-settled in the Rockbridge region—watched the rapid expansion with growing unease.

Among them was John Parsons, a cousin and landholder whose tract bordered the southern perimeter of Henry's holdings. At first, relations between the families remained cordial, grounded in shared heritage and neighborly convention. But as Henry's ambitions accelerated in the 1880s, tensions sharpened.

The catalyst came when Henry proposed constructing a new road to link the upper resort lands with recently acquired acreage. The most practical route would cross a corner of John's property—an idea he vehemently opposed. He argued not only that the road would scar the pastoral landscape, but that it posed a threat to the structural integrity of the Natural Bridge itself.

Word spread that Henry's engineers intended to use dynamite to clear portions of the path, igniting fears that the shock from blasting could damage the arch or destabilize the surrounding terrain. In an area where every stone held ancestral memory and every vista was part of a collective inheritance, such methods struck many as both reckless and emblematic of a troubling shift—from neighbourly stewardship to commercial ambition.

The dispute escalated into a formal impasse.

The dispute between Henry Parsons and his cousin John ultimately culminated in dual court proceedings—one concerning the contested roadway, the other alleging that refuse from Henry's expanding resort operations was being unceremoniously deposited onto John's adjacent land. The litigation drew local attention, as it was rare to see members of the same prominent family clash so publicly over matters of land and legacy. The verdict was split.

John prevailed in the matter of the refuse; the court recognized his claim that waste materials had encroached upon and degraded his property, and awarded him redress. But in the more consequential case concerning the road—Henry's proposed passage through John's land—the judgment fell in Henry's favor. The court upheld his right to proceed, citing broader public utility and the economic benefits attendant to improved access.

Weary from the prolonged strife, John ultimately chose to relinquish his claim, selling the property to Henry. The transaction effectively consolidated Henry's control over the immediate environs of the Natural Bridge, eliminating a critical obstacle to his long-term plans. Wasting no time, Henry incorporated the newly acquired home into his expanding hospitality network. He renovated and enlarged the structure, adding guest accommodations, and formally christened it the Parsons Inn.

9

A Daughter Forsaken

While Henry oversaw the expansion of the grounds and the careful management of its operations, Nellie turned her attention to the moral and intellectual cultivation of their daughters. Removed from the distractions of urban life, the family's residence at the Bridge afforded a degree of privacy and propriety well-suited to their aspirations.

Private tutors instructed their daughters in Latin, French, and composition, while governesses introduced the fundamentals of music, embroidery, and the domestic sciences. Riding was not merely a pastime but a daily discipline, and the bridle paths laid out by Henry through the wooded slopes and meadows became extensions of the classroom—places to learn independence, balance, and grace.

Life at the Bridge was not cloistered, however. The family traveled extensively, seeking both respite and enrichment. Nellie, keenly attuned to the importance of cultural exposure, organized regular visits to New York and Boston, and even crossings to Europe when health, finances, and the tides permitted. These journeys—undertaken at a time when such travel required steamer trunks, calling cards, and weeks of planning—were more than leisure excursions. They reflected a deliberate effort to situate the Parsons daughters within the broader sphere of American and European refinement.

It was during one such sojourn to Boston in the spring of 1889 that Kate Parsons, then twenty-one and already recognized for her draughtsmanship and taste in landscape subjects, was introduced to Mrs. Jeannette Appleton.

A woman of considerable reputation in Bostonian circles, Mrs. Appleton was known not only for her photography but also for her incisive intellect and connections to the city's artistic elite. Her works had been displayed in salons and published in illustrated journals; she possessed both the technical command of the camera and the sensibility of a painter.

Their meeting, though unremarkable in its arrangement— likely facilitated by a mutual acquaintance during a social gathering—would prove consequential. There was a marked affinity between them, rooted perhaps in shared artistic inclination but deepened by temperament and mutual regard. The friendship that followed was swift in its formation and unusually enduring.

To those acquainted with the more theatrical registers of society gossip from a generation past, the name Mrs. Jeannette Appleton—née Ovington—still carried a trace of intrigue, wrapped in the lingering perfume of parlor scandal and sentimentality.

Born into a family of respectable, if not storied lineage, Miss Ovington came of age during a time when marriage was both a strategic venture and a public performance. Her union, while young and photogenic, was with a gentleman far her senior—a settled bachelor of some clubland reputation, whose tastes had long been fixed in the quiet rituals of cigar lounges, late suppers, and a cultivated solitude that did not easily admit the presence of a vivacious bride.

Their early years together, housed within one of the city's more reputable residential hotels, offered a spectacle to their fellow boarders, not for its domestic bliss, but for its conspicuous absence.

The pair, though ostensibly united in law and address, seldom shared a meal or a moment in public. Dining hours passed with separate appearances, and hallways, though narrow, were navigated like foreign frontiers.

It was the peculiar province of elevator attendants and chambermaids to carry the murmurs, which grew into certainties: that quarrels—frequent, sharp, and melodramatic—erupted nightly behind closed doors. The walls, it was said, bore the echoes of accusations hurled like china against plaster, and sighs that lingered into the morning.

Among the lodgers, a collective narrative was spun: Mrs. Appleton, with her wistful eyes and fashionably bobbed hair, came to be viewed as the misunderstood and long-suffering spouse—languid, perhaps a touch dramatic, but wronged nonetheless. Her husband, taciturn and often brusque, earned the role of the imperious brute.

Theirs was not a story of simple estrangement but of mounting incompatibility played in full view of an audience half-shocked, half-entertained.

In time, a legal sundering made official what had long been apparent. After the divorce, the pair became strangers in both practice and propriety—crossing paths without acknowledgment, as though no vows had ever been exchanged.

Yet it would be a mistake to define Mrs. Appleton by misfortune alone. Those who encountered her in later salons or artist societies in Boston and New York spoke not of her former marriage but of her keen aesthetic sense, her unusual sensitivity to light and form, and her facility with the camera lens—a medium then just beginning to claim artistic legitimacy.

Though never again immersed in the rituals of marriage, she cultivated friendships of depth and substance. She was drawn to those of independent spirit, often women like herself who had veered from the expected course and forged new modes of belonging—intellectual, emotional, even artistic. It was then, that Miss Kate Parsons was first introduced to her.

Their acquaintance swiftly matured into a profound alliance, characterized by mutual esteem and intellectual communion. Mrs. Appleton, whose command of photographic artistry was matched only by the quiet fortitude born of personal tribulation, emerged as both mentor and exemplar to the young Parsons. Kate, with her nascent yet ardent artistic vision, invigorated the elder woman's creative endeavors with fresh insight and youthful zeal.

Together, they navigated the era's vibrant artistic milieus—exchanging discourse on aesthetics, the interplay of light and shadow, and the evolving language of visual expression.

As their bond deepened, however, their companionship gradually gave rise to murmurs of concern among those within their social orbit. In an age marked by rigid conventions and cautious whispers, the intensity of their association did not go unnoticed. Yet, even as these concerns mounted, Kate and Mrs. Appleton seemed undeterred.

The summer that followed saw the pair embark upon a conspicuous journey to Europe, returning laden with sumptuous gowns and an array of refined bric-à-brac—tangible emblems of their shared immersion into a world far removed from provincial expectations.

Their conspicuous tastes and independent comportment did little to quell the growing unease among Kate's family.

In response, the patriarch of the Natural Bridge estate sought to invoke the rigor of the law, aiming to curtail Mrs. Appleton's growing influence and to compel the young woman's return to the protective, if confining, sphere of her family.

Yet, Kate remained resolute, spurning the familiarity of home in favor of the austere surroundings of New York boarding houses. There, amidst the city's relentless clamor, she consciously exchanging the serene Virginia landscape for the stark modernity of urban life.

Nearly three years later, in December of 1892, the simmering tensions reached a crescendo with the publication of a striking article in the New York Tribune. This piece, recalling that fateful introduction between Kate and Mrs. Appleton, cast their relationship in a sensational light, stirring unease far beyond their immediate circle. The article's provocative tone and insinuations thrust the Parsons family into an uncomfortable spotlight, challenging the carefully maintained decorum that had long defined their social standing.

"BEAUTY HELD IN HYPNOTIC FETTERS. That's What the Friends of Miss Katherine Parsons Say Keeps Her Away from Her Father and Family.

MRS. APPLETON'S STRANGE INFLUENCE The Daughter of the Owner of the Natural Bridge and a Leader Among the "F.F.V.'s" the Alleged Victim of This Power. Other Means Having Failed, a Grief-Stricken Parent Will Take Legal Measures to Recover His Child.

DENIALS AND RECRIMINATION If the stories of perfectly reputable and reliable people are to be credited, it is nothing less than the hypnotic gift which has blasted the hitherto perfect happiness of a happy Southern home. It has torn a beautiful and accomplished daughter from her aged parents and caused her to cast in her lot with a woman who two years ago was a stranger to her.

It has made a frantic wanderer of an aged father who had sought for a year and thus far unsuccessfully to break the spell which binds his child in fetters more strong than iron or steel. It has completely warped that daughter's heart so that she no longer feels impulse of natural affection, but regards her parents and sisters with aversion."

The narrative surrounding Mrs. Appleton's ascendancy in Kate Parsons's life took a complex turn when it emerged that she and Henry Parsons had, at one time, been collaborators in a commercial undertaking of artistic ambition. The project in question concerned the production of elaborately staged photographic views of the Natural Bridge.

Mrs. Appleton was commissioned to capture the site's grandeur on glass plates, with an understanding that the resulting prints would be sold, and any financial gains divided equally between herself and her husband, Colonel Appleton.

But the venture, like many idealistic enterprises, proved fragile in execution.

Sales faltered, disagreements over financial accounts surfaced, and soon the original spirit of cooperation gave way to discord. Allegations of withheld proceeds and unfulfilled promises began to circulate, eventually leading to an open rupture between Mrs. Appleton and the Parsons family. This falling out, described by one observer as "irreparable," effectively severed all ties between the two parties—save one.

To her family's dismay, Kate refused to dissolve her relationship with the woman now at odds with her parents. By then, Mrs. Appleton was living apart from her husband in Manhattan, having cultivated a reputation for living on her own terms. It was into her solitary household that Kate moved—an act regarded by her relations not merely as a lapse in judgment, but as an outright rejection of the values in which she had been raised.

Their European retreat had emboldened this fact further. Kate returned with an air not only of cosmopolitan polish but of defiance. No longer content to play the dutiful daughter, she appeared instead as a woman increasingly sure of her autonomy—and of her allegiance. The refinement gained abroad had not softened her to familial appeals; if anything, it seemed to have hardened her resolve.

Meanwhile, Mrs. Appleton, unbothered by the growing backlash, made no effort to disguise their domestic arrangement. Visitors to her West Side residence noted Kate's presence with unease—though whether as companion, protégé, or something more, few dared say aloud.

Given the nature of such uncertainties, efforts to reclaim Kate intensified.

Her family's entreaties, once rooted in paternal sorrow and maternal longing, took on the tone of desperation. Letters, unanswered. Appeals, rebuffed. Eventually, Henry employed legal counsel to establish contact, a final attempt to penetrate the fortified reserve into which Kate had withdrawn. The attorney, upon returning from Oyster Bay, reported that access had been closely managed. He had not, at any point, been granted private conversation with the young woman; Mrs. Appleton was present throughout, a persistent figure in both literal and metaphorical proximity.

No resolution followed.

Kate, unmoved by familial grief or public scrutiny, made clear through intermediaries that her course had been fixed. In the months that ensued, this posture hardened into a kind of domestic exile. She and Mrs. Appleton withdrew from the social circuits that once defined their respective lives, establishing themselves within the quiet but ever-observant world of New York boarding houses.

The first of these residences, situated within the genteel but closely surveilled world of Manhattan lodging establishments, proved inhospitable to their continued stay. Though neither woman engaged in overt impropriety, their mode of living—marked by an unusual exclusivity and intensity of companionship—soon gave rise to disquiet among fellow boarders. Their comportment, described in contemporary accounts as a "reputation for singularity of behavior," ultimately led to their quiet dismissal from the premises.

Still determined, the pair relocated to more commodious quarters elsewhere in the city. There, too, their arrival was heralded by an immediate stir: Kate and Mrs. Appleton appeared daily in lavish attire, their wardrobes echoing the refinement and excess of continental tastes—gowns of velvet and silk, elaborately pinned coiffures, gloves of kid leather, and parasols embroidered with monograms.

Their manners were irreproachable, their bearing genteel, and yet it was precisely this air of distinction—combined with their impenetrable bond—that provoked equal parts admiration and suspicion among fellow residents.

It was during this period that a reporter from the *New York Tribune*, pursuing the human contours of the unfolding drama, conducted an interview with Mrs. Briggs, the matron of one such boarding house. In her remarks, Mrs. Briggs noted a growing unease regarding the dynamic she observed between the two women. "I was convinced," she stated with unambiguous concern, "that Miss Kate Parsons was under some influence which the young lady herself could scarcely account for."

Mrs. Briggs, clearly affected by what she perceived as a subtle domination, elaborated upon her repeated efforts to engage Kate in private conversation. These attempts, she claimed, were consistently thwarted by Mrs. Appleton, who objected—often with palpable vehemence—to Kate's momentary separation from her company. "Mrs. Appleton," she said, "flatly objected to Miss Parsons leaving her even for an instant, and thus balked all my efforts."

Such incidents were not confined to private encounters. One episode, witnessed by several boarders, occurred at luncheon, when Kate—soft-spoken and reflective—referred to her father in affectionate terms. According to Mrs. Briggs, the response was swift and incendiary. Mrs. Appleton, consumed with ire, rose from her place and declared that she was "astonished Miss Parsons should dare to speak of that man." The vitriol of the outburst left no doubt as to her desire to sever Kate's filial affections entirely.

In the weeks that followed, whispers gave way to open speculation. The atmosphere within the house grew untenable, colored by conjecture and punctuated by wary glances. The "gossip about them became so rampant," she later told the *Tribune*, "that I was left with no alternative but to request their departure."

So once more, the pair moved on—discreetly, deliberately, and always together.

Their next address was a modest boarding establishment at No. 18 East Twenty-eighth Street, where the Tribune correspondent, drawn by the rising tide of rumor, soon sought them out. It was there, behind a closed parlor door, that Mrs. Appleton was directly confronted with the most sensational accusation yet: that she had exercised a mesmeric—or as some whispered, "hypnotic"—dominion over Miss Parsons's will.

Mrs. Appleton, no stranger to social rebuke, received the charge with cool disdain.

She attributed the slander not to substance, but to vengeance—an unfortunate outgrowth, she contended, of a fractured association with their former landlady, Mrs. Briggs.

Pressed for clarity, she offered a narrative laced with grievance and social injury. Upon their arrival at No. 68 West Thirty-ninth Street, she explained, Mrs. Briggs had extended the warmth of fellowship. In time, this amiability turned opportunistic: a request was made for funds to improve the property. Mrs. Appleton, unable to comply directly, turned to her circle for aid. While willing to assist her personally, her friends hesitated at underwriting a stranger. This rebuff, it seemed, wounded Mrs. Briggs's pride, and thereafter her demeanor grew cold.

"Then, as I am a woman who speaks as I think," Mrs. Appleton told the reporter. "I candidly told Mrs. Briggs that I no longer held her in the esteem I had formerly felt for her. When we announced that we were going to leave the house, things were made decidedly unpleasant for us, and Mrs. Briggs started stories about us."

Miss Parsons, composed and measured, endorsed this account without embellishment. She further observed that her father's continued attempts to reclaim her—fruitless though they had proven—might have fueled the wider narrative. It was, perhaps, easier for the public to imagine enchantment than to accept her voluntary separation from the sphere of familial duty.

"My family," said Miss Parsons, "wished me to remain at home, but I would not have there the advantages in studying art that I require, and for this reason I am living in this city. My father, in Boston several years ago, introduced Mrs. Appleton to me. We have been close friends ever since; but as for Mrs. Appleton's exerting an undue influence over me it is absolutely ridiculous. I am of age and perfectly competent to take care of myself."

When every avenue of reconciliation had narrowed into silence, when the appeals of kinship met only a cloistered resolve, Henry Parsons committed his sorrow not to action, but to paper.

The result was a private lament, mournful in tone, restrained in form, addressed to his wife and surviving daughters. It bore the traces of a man reckoning not only with loss, but with a kind of spiritual bewilderment:

"No cable will come back—no letter—no sign of life or death. She will succeed—she will become distinguished, but she will belong to the world—another, never again to us. This I cannot yet comprehend. But we shall live and our dear house will draw close—three beautiful talented daughters, loyal & loving will give us comfort. There are no flowers—no last word—no consolation in life or death.

God bless you, my dear wife, and Maud, and Gretchen."

Thus, the household settled back into its old symmetry— one daughter absent, two remaining, each carrying forward her father's hope that loyalty might still triumph where affection alone had failed.

Life, persistent in its motion, did not pause for grief.

With the passage of months, the Parsons name—once synonymous with Southern rectitude and ancestral honor—began to appear in a different register. What had once been spoken with deference in Richmond drawing rooms and on courthouse steps now surfaced in parlors with a hush, accompanied by glances and elliptical phrases.

The scandal, propelled by gossip columns and sensational broadsheets, had done its corrosive work. Not through vulgarity or criminality, but through something far more insidious to the era's sensibilities: impropriety without explanation, allegiance without sanction, and a young woman's refusal to repent.

Henry, for all his military distinction and public service, found his family's name increasingly tethered to that of Mrs. Appleton—a woman whose reputation, once merely curious, had hardened into notoriety. Doors that once opened easily now required renewed negotiation. Invitations once taken for granted arrived belatedly, if at all.

It was in this climate—of mounting reputational erosion—that Henry was forced to reckon not simply with loss, but with responsibility. He could no longer afford to orbit the question of Kate's fate as a father alone. The broader claims of his household demanded precedence. Maud and Gretchen remained under his roof, their futures still unwritten. To allow Kate's defiance to overshadow their prospects was a dereliction he could not countenance.

Henry's carefully maintained evasions—casting his daughter's prolonged absence as a dutiful visit to an ailing relative—had done little to quell suspicion or restore order. With the narrative unraveling and few recourses remaining, he turned once more to the public forum. Thus, with a stoicism forged in war and a pragmatism refined through decades of patriarchal stewardship, Henry penned another letter to the *New York Tribune*. It began as:

"Whether or not Katharine is attending an invalid, either with or without the consent of her parents, can in no manner concern the public."

It was a rhetorical pivot: by rejecting the public's right to pry into his daughter's whereabouts or motives, Henry sought to reframe the situation as one of inappropriate speculation, rather than moral collapse. Yet, beneath its composed tone, the line also reveals his growing resignation—an acknowledgment that the family's internal crisis had slipped irrevocably into the public domain.

He proceeded to repudiate, in the firmest terms, a litany of circulating allegations: that he had ever entered into any business arrangement with Mrs. Appleton; that his daughter had, at any point, accompanied that lady overseas; that he himself had undertaken any covert journey to New York or Boston with the aim of securing Kate's return; or that he had retained the services of legal counsel or hired agents to conduct surveillance, initiate proceedings, or otherwise assert dominion over his daughter's personal affairs.

Each charge, he insisted, was without foundation— fabrications born of idle speculation and public appetite for scandal.

"I have never been denied access to my daughter, nor has she ever returned my letters unanswered. My daughter is not estranged from her father. It may also be well to say that I do not recognize in myself the frantic searcher after my lost child, but

happy in my home, with a father's full measure of pride and faith in my daughter Katharine. I concede to her absolute freedom to follow her inclinations and convictions, knowing that she in influenced by conscientious and self-sacrificing purposes in every act of hers, and I hope that these definite aims will account for her friends and protect her from further public criticism."

In the surviving copy of the letter preserved among Maud Parsons's private papers, subtle yet telling emendations reveal a fracture between public narrative and private truth. A series of lines—where Henry had initially insisted he had never been denied access to his daughter, nor had any of his letters gone unanswered—were carefully struck through.

A paragraph extolling the "full measure of paternal pride" was similarly excised, as were subsequent phrases concerning Kate's circle of companions. The deliberate nature of these redactions suggests not editorial refinement but familial dissent.

Maud, perhaps unwilling to let her father's narrative stand unchallenged in perpetuity, had rendered visible the artifice. In ink and strikethrough, she left behind a quiet testimony: that Henry Parsons, for all his eloquence and moral certainty, had not spoken in full truth.

There was no closing scene, no moment of reckoning to tie the ends neatly. The absence of drama, in its own way, became the most telling feature of the final chapter between Kate and her family. She never saw her father, again. In January of 1894, she and Mrs. Appleton departed the United States quietly. Behind them trailed a wake of scandal, speculation, severed ties and looming tension that would inevitably result in her father's brutal murder.

Kate remained abroad for the rest of her life, casting roots in the cultivated salons and ateliers of Europe. Her paintings—elegant, introspective, and distinctly modern—earned her quiet esteem within expatriate and aristocratic circles. Though never the subject of wide renown, she carved a place for herself in a world of her own making.

In the twilight years of her life, Kate Parsons stood at the threshold of nobility. Her engagement to Count Alexander von Gerdorff—scion of an old Austro-German lineage and son of the imperial chamberlain—promised entrance into a world of titles, estates, and formal distinction. It was, on paper, a culmination: the orphaned Southern belle turned European artist, poised now to ascend into aristocracy.

But beneath the veneer of continental success lay a more profound and irreparable loss. Kate had won status, but forfeited belonging. The nobility she was to join would never supplant the family she had left behind. She had traded blood for freedom, and kin for the promise of self-determination. And in doing so, she left behind not only her name, but the very concept of home.

She died just months before the marriage, the alliance with Count von Gerdorff remained a future suspended and then irrevocably lost.

In the weeks following her death, a brief but poignant tribute appeared in the local Massachusetts newspaper. It was penned by her sister Grace—a woman otherwise known for her reserve, now compelled to grapple with this complex legacy:

"Young hands that fashioned beauty with flaming skill; Tired hands that blundered with life's promise, creased and still; Giving

away love, youth and fame so royally. Dead hands I kiss too late; yet your brave spirit seems To wave a dim farewell across the alien sea of dreams."

These lines—elegant and restrained—spoke more eloquently than any obituary. They revealed not only admiration for Kate's talent, but also sorrow, bewilderment, and an unresolved sense of loss. The juxtapositions encapsulated the family's divided view of her: brilliant, willful, and ultimately estranged. It was an epitaph not just for a life lost, but for a relationship never mended.

She was laid to rest in a cemetery outside Florence, among other expatriates and artists who had also sought beauty abroad. Her estate—comprising paintings of undeniable merit, a cache of fine furnishings, and jewelry acquired in more gilded days— remained unclaimed by her kin. No one traveled to Italy to sort her belongings. No legal emissary was dispatched. The objects, like the artist herself, were left behind—ornate, valuable, but unwanted.

Part 3
The Final Tragedy

"When they see good men thus try to shield red-handed murderers from paying the penalty of their crimes, as far as testifying to character is concerned, what does that amount to?"

1

The Inquiry Begins

It is a cruel paradox of history that the daughter who sowed discord within her father's household should also be the inadvertent catalyst for the tragedy that would ultimately claim his life. Such was the somber irony that marked the Parsons family's descent into turmoil—an unraveling woven as much by personal grievances as by the inexorable currents of circumstance.

As former president of the Chesapeake and Ohio Railroad, Henry Parsons remained a respected figure in Virginia's civic and industrial life. Though he had stepped down from formal leadership, the railroad continued to honor him with passes for himself and his immediate family—an enduring courtesy for years of devoted service.

Two years prior, Kate Parsons and her family became estranged. She boarded a train with the purpose of going from Natural Bridge to Richmond. It was a courtesy Kate Parsons had relied upon many times, and on a spring afternoon in 1889, she stepped aboard the train with every expectation that tradition would carry her through once more. But when the conductor approached and asked for her ticket, Kate reached into her reticule and realized, too late, that she had left her pass behind.

She gave her name, invoked her father's legacy, and expected leniency. However, the Conductor Thomas A. Goodman remained unmoved. He listened without hostility, but insisted on fare. Regulations, he said, required consistency.

Kate returned home indignant. To her, the fare wasn't the issue—it was the insult, the sense of being treated like a stranger in a system her father had once governed. She recounted the episode to her parents, and her mother quickly took up her cause. Together, they pressed Henry to respond. He was not a man easily provoked, but in the sanctity of his own home, faced with the wounded pride of his daughter and the quiet insistence of his wife, he relented.

His letter to the railroad's headquarters was respectful and restrained. He expressed no grievance, only concern that the handling of the matter had overlooked long-established ties.

The reply came swiftly.

The railroad expressed appreciation for his past service, but affirmed that Goodman had acted within protocol. And that, by most accounts, would have been the end of it.

Yet, it was not.

Over the following year, quiet tensions surfaced in encounters between the Parsons family and Goodman. None were dramatic, but they were persistent. Accounts reached the Colonel—some firsthand, others from friends or local travelers—of Goodman's stiffness with passengers, his brusque tone, and an air of officiousness that, though not explicitly unkind, seemed to ignore the nuances of decorum long expected of men in public-facing roles.

Parsons, steeped in the customs of a more deferential age, believed that institutions flourished not through rigid rule but through discernment, where respect and reason walked in tandem. And while he had never sought to leverage his name for undue privilege, he understood the difference between rules rightly enforced and authority applied without temper.

By March of 1894, he had seen enough to warrant formal notice. He wrote once more—this time addressed to General Manager G.W. Stevens.

"Dear Sir

Some time ago I called your official attention to what I deemed a discourteous treatment of my daughter [Kate] by a conductor of yours named Thomas A. Goodman; however, stating that he did not violate your rules, except by his cruelty of manners, nothing came of it. Since then, my principal inconvenience comes from the fact that my wife has refused to ride or allow any lady friends to ride—unattended upon the train when he was on, if it could be avoided, and this has resulted in much telegraphing and changing of plans.

About the time of the first occurrence, I learned of a similar instance of treatment of a banker in Richmond, who felt and yet feels, as much as I do. Two other instances came to my attention—one of a gentleman from Harrisonburg and one of a gentleman from San Francisco, who was greatly offended, and one of whom I believe sent in a protest. But in every case, he kept within the rules.

Henry did not dwell on the past incident involving Kate, but described a pattern of conduct that, in his view, merited attention. His words carried no personal malice, but rather the concern of a man who feared that the railroad's public face had grown indifferent to the very people it was built to serve.

Among the charges leveled against Goodman, one of the most concerning was a claim suggesting he had attempted to involve the stationmaster's wife, Mrs. Staples, in some improper manner—an allegation that, if true, would have cast a serious shadow not only over Goodman's professional conduct but also his personal honor.

Therefore, Henry suggested, cautiously but deliberately, that Conductor Goodman's temperament might be ill-suited to his role. It was a grave charge for the time—one that prompted Stevens to refer the matter to Superintendent J.B. Doyle for internal review.

Goodman was summoned, presented with the claims, and invited to respond. He denied the accusations categorically and, by some accounts, even welcomed a formal investigation.

Whether out of genuine confidence or indignation, he maintained that his actions were in keeping with company policy and that any perception of impropriety was unfounded.

In his reply dated June 26, Goodman vigorously denied the accusations. He expressed incredulity that the so-called "Richmond banker," the "gentleman from Harrisonburg," or the "gentleman from San Francisco" had ever lodged complaints. He repudiated the remaining allegations as fabrications, save for an incident in which he had been forced to remove a woman of questionable reputation near Salt Petre Cave. Moreover, he firmly denied any misconduct involving the stationmaster's wife.

Goodman's vigorous defense was not merely a reflection of professional pride; it was the voice of a man whose entire livelihood—and the welfare of his family—rested upon his reputation.

Thomas A. Goodman, about forty-five years of age and a native son of Powhatan County, was more than just an employee of the Chesapeake and Ohio Railroad. He was a husband and father to six children, all residing in Richmond, whose stability depended on his steady employment. Having dedicated eighteen years to the railroad, save for a two-year period on the Pacific coast, Goodman embodied the working-class spirit of late nineteenth-century Virginia—resilient, dutiful, and acutely aware of the consequences that any blemish on his name could bring.

Now, with everything precariously poised, Goodman grasped the gravity of his situation. Every word, every gesture, every decision could tip the scales against him.

2

Crimson on the Hardwood

Clifton Forge stirred with the heat of late June, the scent of coal smoke and creosote thickening in the humid dusk. Trains groaned to a halt beneath iron gantries, and the voices of porters drifted out from the freight yards. Just up the rise from the platform, where the lamplight tilted long across the wooden sidewalks, the Gladys Inn stood in the fading light like a sentinel of the rails—gabled, weatherworn, and unmistakably tied to the pulse of the railroad.

Inside, its walls held the residue of conversations not meant for ledgers. Men passed through the doors weary from long hauls, their uniforms streaked with soot, their collars limp with sweat. Some came to rest; others came to listen, or be seen. The inn, after all, was no ordinary hostelry—it was railroad property, a waystation not only for men and meals but for matters of consequence.

On the evening of June 28, 1894, Conductor Goodman entered not with the gait of a man retreating into routine, but with a purpose that gave his steps a certain stiffness. There was no mistaking it: *he was watching the doors.*

From the first wan light breaking over the stone escarpments of Natural Bridge that morning, Goodman's course had been set. His movements bore the pattern not of a workingman completing his rounds, but of a man tracing a thread with quiet resolve.

At the depot in Natural Bridge, he had stepped aside from his duties long enough to pose a single, deliberate question: *Had Colonel Henry Parsons passed through?* The query, though offered plainly, carried with it a tension beneath the surface— measured, premeditated, and undoubtedly personal.

As the hours unspooled and the day folded into the heavy warmth of evening, Goodman disembarked in Clifton Forge and made his way toward the Gladys Inn. There, before attending to any supper or room, he inquired again. The repetition of the question—first along the tracks, then within the walls of the company's own inn—marked not mere curiosity, but pursuit.

By the time he seated himself near the windows, each creak of the floorboards, each silhouette at the door, pulled his gaze. And beneath that steady watchfulness was the quiet gravity of weeks gone tense—accusations whispered along official lines, his name passed like folded paper from hand to hand.

Whatever had been brewing, it had now narrowed to a point. This was not the hour of chance encounters. It was the threshold of something long in the making.

But Henry did not come.

By half past eight, the last evening train had departed with a sigh of steam and the clatter of couplings, and still there had been no sign of the man Goodman sought. The inn's register remained unsigned by that particular hand, and the bench by the hearth, where men sometimes loitered for news or whiskey, held only a pair of sleeping porters.

Goodman stayed downstairs long after most had gone to bed. He was not a man easily given to rest when a matter went unresolved. Though outwardly composed, there was a growing tautness in his silence, like wire wound too tightly.

No announcement was made. No carriage rolled in. At last, sometime near midnight, Goodman retired to his room.

He remained awake in his room well into the small hours. When the clock in the parlor struck half-past four, he rose, washed, and—habitually, as he would later testify—retrieved the revolver kept beneath his pillow.

Goodman was not, by temperament or custom, the sort of man who armed himself lightly. In his eighteen years on the line, he had encountered drunks, vagrants, and the occasional temper boiling over in a railcar, but his authority had never needed the reinforcement of a firearm. Conductors, after all, were expected to manage chaos with civility, not steel.

Yet, in the growing pressure, he had begun to feel that civility alone might no longer suffice. There was no second thought. No tremor in the hand, no pause to reconsider.

In his own words, recorded in testimony and published in The Richmond Dispatch not long after, he described the moment with the plainness of a man certain of his course:

"After dressing, I took my pistol from under my pillow and put it in my pocket. My train was to leave at 8:30, and I got down stairs a little before 7, put my little satchel on the hat-rack, and going into the dining-room ... ordered my breakfast, and after waiting a minute or two, I heard someone in the lobby clearing his throat as to spit and walk over toward the fireplace."

The sound itself was unremarkable—a clearing of the throat, the shuffle of boot leather on polished pine. In any other setting, it might have passed without notice, absorbed into the background murmur of a railroad inn waking to its morning rituals. But on this particular morning, it struck Conductor Goodman with an uncanny precision.

"I happened to look up, and partly saw through the door, a man whom I took to be Colonel Parsons."

He asked Henry Moody, the dining-room waiter, to confirm what he already suspected. The answer came promptly: yes—it was him.

In that moment, no hesitation stirred in him. He stood. He retrieved the letter from his pocket—the same one he had carried through two towns, the same one whose ink had already altered the course of his life.

"I believe I'll go out to see him." He said more to himself than to Moody.

"When I got in the lobby, I saw Colonel Parsons in the office. I got my satchel off the hat-rack and took from it the copy of the letter. As I replaced the satchel, Colonel Parsons came out of the office and stood in front of the porch, looking partly out of the door and partly on the lawn. I had the letter in my hand and walked up to him."

Without raising his voice or disturbing the calm of the room, Goodman closed the distance between them. Henry had not seemed to notice him. Whether out of distraction or deliberate indifference, it could not be said. Intent on making himself known, Goodman pushed further—not with hostility, but with the urgency of unspoken consequence—and placed his hand on the lapel of Parsons' coat.

"Colonel, come out to the door, I have a letter I want you to look at."

Henry turned at the sound of his name, his eyes narrowing with guarded curiosity. Whatever familiarity Goodman had expected to find in the Colonel's face did not surface. The glance Henry offered was impersonal, opaque—a careful assessment rather than recognition. If he knew Goodman, he gave no sign. If he understood the nature of what was unfolding, he concealed it well.

Goodman, watching, interpreted the delay not as disbelief, but as confirmation. In his own later account, he would describe that pause not merely as evasion, but as a second kind of betrayal—a refusal to grant even the decency of acknowledgement.

The moment held.

Henry looked down—not at Goodman, but at the paper. He knew it well. He had written it, or enough of it to recognize its content. Whatever confidence had fueled its drafting now seemed to hesitate in the light of morning. What calculations passed behind his eyes cannot be precisely known, but something—perhaps the desire to avoid a public escalation in the lobby, or a belief that he could still speak the situation down—tipped the balance.

He straightened slowly, eyes fixed now on Goodman, and nodded once. Without a word, he stepped away from the hearth.

Outside, the first true heat of the day had begun to gather along the boards of the porch. A faint shimmer clung to the street beyond, where the outlines of passing figures blurred briefly in the rising glare. Henry moved without speaking, his pace deliberate, his expression unreadable. He did not turn to look at Goodman until they had crossed the threshold of the inn and reached the shade beneath the cornice.

There, in the muffled quiet just beyond the earshot of others, Goodman extended the folded page. Henry took the paper, holding it for a moment in both hands as if weighing it. His eyes traced the lines without haste. Whatever familiarity he found on the page was not acknowledged aloud. No apology followed. No disclaimer. Only a faint narrowing of the eyes, and a shift of the jaw that might have marked tension—or resolve.

Goodman broke the silence.

"Are you the author of this letter," he asked, *"this ruinous letter, which is not only calculated to ruin me, but to destroy the peace and happiness of my family?"*

The Colonel did not answer immediately. He held the paper a moment longer, as though its ink were still drying, then let it fall—unceremoniously. It drifted down between them and landed against the toe of Goodman's boot.

"You nor your family were considered. Let's keep personalities out of it." Henry said, the words clipped, devoid of feeling. The

line might have been intended to end the exchange—to shut it down cleanly and move on—but in context, it carried a weight that went far beyond indifference. It negated everything Goodman had come to demand: recognition, responsibility, and the smallest ounce of regret.

Henry made to turn back, his head already shifting away. But Goodman stepped forward, voice calm but with unmistakable firmness. *"Stop,"* he said. *"You must retract that."*

His opponent halted. Slowly, he rotated back to face him, brows arched in a look that skirted the line between disbelief and derision.

"What?" he asked—not as a question, but as a dare.

Henry did not linger to answer. His face closed like a shutter. Whatever retort had briefly sparked behind his eyes, he chose to swallow it, pivoting on his heel toward the inn's entrance. Goodman shadowed him step for step, the distance between them too slight to suggest retreat, yet too precise to seem rash.

They passed once more beneath the portico, leaving the gauze of morning light behind them, and entered the lobby—its hush somehow more oppressive now, thick with an expectation no one yet named. The clock struck the quarter hour with a hollow chime. Neither man acknowledged it.

Inside, the room had resumed its quiet rhythms. The same waiter, Henry Moody, moved between tables. A housecat dozed along the edge of a windowsill. Outside the inn's register book, there remained no obvious record that any private matter had disturbed the peace of the hour.

But that peace was an illusion.

Henry's right arm moved back, low, and behind him. To anyone else, it might have looked like a man reaching to adjust the hem of his coat. But to Goodman, still keyed by weeks of unease, it suggested something more.

He would later claim that the Colonel's hand moved with "deliberate intent," that it was not the reflex of surprise but the practiced motion of someone reaching for a weapon. And though no pistol was ever drawn by Henry that morning, the impression was enough.

Goodman slipped the revolver from beneath his coat, his right hand cupping the grip, his left arm crossing to absorb the recoil.

A sharp crackle fractured the tranquil air. Henry jerked, his shoulders pulsing—but he remained upright. The second and third rounds followed in immediate succession, each one echoing with sharpened purpose.

Henry, wounded but unbowed, lunged forward. His hands sought Goodman's wrist with desperate urgency. He gasped the name "Mr. White! Mr. White!"—the hotel manager, his voice taut with desperation as he clutched Goodman's shooting arm with both hands.

For a fleeting moment, confrontation turned to struggle. The Colonel's fingers twined around Goodman's wrist, a clash of flesh and iron. The lobby's register book, padded with early entries, lay forgotten. Waitstaff froze mid-motion. The ticking of the wall clock was muffled beneath the surge of tension.

Goodman did not pause. His right hand, suddenly unbound, lashed out not again at Henry's chest but upward. The pistol rose with his arm and discharged once more. This final shot rang near his temple, thunderous and unintended. Physicians would later say it was careless or reflexive, but in that suspended moment, it was *decisive.*

Henry fell.

He crumpled beside a mahogany armchair—his coat brushing the faded upholstery—eyes closed before the boards could touch his cheek. A dark stain blossomed across his chest and spread swiftly toward his legs, staining the polished wood with a slow certainty.

The instant swallowed itself. Silence followed, barbed and dense.

Goodman stood motionless above the fallen man. Smoke lingered faintly around the muzzle; iron scent hung heavy in the air. He flipped open the revolver's chamber, each spent shell tumbling out with a mechanical tap onto the hardwood floor— like coins dropped at a ledger's close.

There was no recoil, no collapse of form or face. No eyes wet with remorse. Across his features, only an exhaustion deeper than grief.

Behind him, Mr. White emerged from the office, jaw slack, face paled. Other guests and staff hovered at the edges, lips parted, hands trembling. Somebody gasped. Another cleared his throat, uncertain. Outside, a murmur had begun to swell: hurried footsteps, a distant shout for the marshal, the key rattle of a front door opening wide.

And yet inside, Goodman remained stationary. *He had just killed someone.*

The reality sank in.

Then, before the call for help could fully register, he made his move.

He stepped lightly over Parsons's prone form and brushed past the gathering crowd, their expressions caught between horror and disbelief. The lobby doors swung open, and Goodman, hair dusted with chalk-white from the inn's clapboards, emerged onto the sun-struck portico.

He had escaped.

*****

Colonel Parsons was carefully lifted onto a canvas cot and carried into the privacy of the inn's front office. Dr. R. D. Miller, the Chesapeake & Ohio Railroad's appointed surgeon, arrived moments later, his leather medical bag in hand and his expression a blend of urgency and solemnity. Staff members fell silent as he bent to examine Parsons's wounds.

For forty-five minutes, Miller worked—inspecting wounds, issuing soft directives, attempting compressions where pressure might briefly resist the inevitable. But by the turn of the hour, the prognosis was no longer in question.

Colonel Henry C. Parsons was declared dead.

His body, still warm, lay arranged on the cot beneath a borrowed quilt, but the force that had animated him—a man who'd once commanded regiments and walked with the quiet gravity of consequence—was gone. In its place lingered the remains of an unresolved quarrel and a silence far heavier than death alone could account for.

In the aftermath, Mr. Martin, the hotel clerk who had been stationed just behind the registration desk, was questioned first. He had witnessed the shooting but could offer little beyond that. The entire affair had transpired in a storm of motion and thunderous report. What words passed between the men outside, or even inside, just before the shots rang out, were lost beneath the commotion.

The blood in the lobby had begun to dull and turn, congealing into a dark patch that no amount of water could easily erase. The guests whispered. The manager moved like a man in half-light, his face pale with recognition—not just of what had happened, but of how little could now be undone.

No weapon was recovered from Parsons. His coat was unbuttoned by Miller's hand; his vest, undisturbed. In the left pocket, they found only a folded handkerchief and a torn page—the last remnant of the dispute that had drawn blood that morning. Whatever gesture Goodman had claimed to see—a threat perceived—was, in the final measure, untrue.

By nightfall, the hotel manager ordered black bunting draped over the entrance. A telegram was dispatched to Mrs. Parsons at Natural Bridge Station. Within the hour, arrangements had been made for a private locomotive to be sent northward. The crew was instructed to wait on no timetable, carry no other passengers.

The next day, at precisely 1:15 p.m., the whistle of an unscheduled locomotive pierced the heat. It pulled into the

Clifton Forge depot slowly, its steel frame sighing under the burden of grief it had been sent to bear. From its single car emerged Mrs. Nellie Parsons and her daughters—Grace and Maud. They descended without assistance, their faces pale, veiled, unreadable.

Word of their arrival had traveled faster than the train. A hush had settled over the depot; storekeepers along the tracks stood in their doorframes, hats in hand. A florist's boy stopped mid-pedal. Even the horses tethered nearby seemed subdued, swishing their tails in the quiet.

Mrs. Parsons entered the carriage that had been sent to receive them, not with haste, but with a composed, almost ceremonial gravity. She did not weep. Her gloved hand rested on the doorframe as if steadying herself against the final confirmation of what the telegram had already declared. Beside her, the girls sat in silence, their postures stiff with effort. They were not yet old enough to carry such grief—but here they were, learning how.

At the inn, the blood had been scrubbed away. Though the foyer's boards gleamed beneath layers of lye and water, a residual stain—deep as wine and just as stubborn—persisted beneath the varnish like a memory etched into wood. Guests sidestepped the spot without speaking of it. Mr. White, once brisk and affable, now moved as if under a private sentence—his gait halting, his voice diminished, his hands perpetually fussing at the seams of his waistcoat as though wringing out that morning's horror.

Behind the closed door of the front office, Colonel Henry C. Parsons lay beneath a tightly drawn woollen shroud. The room was austere, the shutters half-drawn, the air marked by the faint scent of carbolic and wilted flowers. Dr. R.D. Miller stood in the corner like a mourner who had no words left to offer. His medical bag rested unopened at his feet. Nothing remained to be done.

When Mrs. Parsons entered, the stillness grew tense, like a held breath. She approached her husband's form with the dignity of someone long acquainted with silence and sorrow. Her gloved hand reached forward—not to embrace, not to confirm—but to graze the edge of the covering, a touch as ceremonial as it was bereft.

Behind her, Grace and Maud lingered at the threshold. The younger leaned into the older's side, their faces pale beneath the brims of their travel bonnets, unsure whether to cross the line between the living and the dead.

*****

On Sunday, July 1st, under a blistering noon sun, Colonel Parsons was laid to rest in High Pointe Cemetery. The town turned out in full, their mourning shaded by parasols and pressed linen. At the head of the cortege walked six young girls, daughters of men who had served the Colonel in rail yards and militia lines alike. Dressed in white muslin and ribbons dulled by heat, they carried lilies in loose bundles and dropped them at careful intervals, a slow trail of petals softening the path to the grave.

Behind them came the hearse—its black drapery flanking polished wood like a military standard at half-mast. Then the family carriage, shuttered and silent. The hotel staff followed, then the townsfolk on foot and in wagons.

Some had come from distant junctions, summoned by telegram and memory. Others had arrived unbidden, drawn by obligation, or loyalty, or the desire to see for themselves the resting place of a man who had once seemed larger than the boundaries of a single town.

The service, held beneath the outstretched boughs of a weathered oak, was spare and without flourish. The minister, voice tired with age, offered no fevered liturgy. Instead, he spoke of the transient nature of industry and ambition, of men who shape things only to be shaped in turn by fate. He did not invoke Goodman's name, nor did he speak of the killing. What he offered was simpler—a reflection on labor, mortality, and the inevitable surrender of the flesh to dust.

As the casket descended into the earth, a breeze rose from the south, rustling the leaves overhead and sending a ribbon from Grace's bonnet adrift. One lily, caught in the wind, slipped through the air and came to rest atop the lowering casket before it vanished below.

The mourners began to disperse. Some bowed their heads. Others turned quietly toward their carriages, the solemnity of the hour retreating into the rustle of dresses and the creak of wooden wheels.

But Nellie Parsons did not move.

She stood at the edge of the grave, veiled and unmoving. Her gaze was not fixed on the grave itself but somewhere beyond it— across the cresting hills, as if looking for the point where sky and soil folded into one another. She remained until the last clod of earth had been tamped down and the stone marker laid flat above the soil.

No word had yet surfaced of Goodman's whereabouts. He had vanished into the American wilderness—flesh and motive alike slipping beyond the net of law. Rumors trailed in his wake, but no sighting could be confirmed, no justice neatly drawn.

And so, the season turned.

In the meadows beyond the cemetery walls, the cicadas sang their ancient chorus, unperturbed. The world did not stop. But Clifton Forge had been altered—subtly, irrevocably. Something had torn loose beneath its surface that summer, and no amount of time, nor prayer, nor sweat from the innkeeper's hand, could fully scrub it clean.

3

Sweet Surrender

In the wake of five gunshots and a collapsing man, Captain William Goodman did not abscond into the mountain passes or vanish down the iron lines that webbed the Valley. He did not plead confusion, nor did he wait for the knock at his door. Instead, he did the one thing few expected in the wake of a killing so public: he gave himself over.

Shortly after noon on June 29th, having walked the length of the platform with measured step, Goodman entered the Clifton Forge depot—not as a conductor reporting for duty, but as a man prepared to be unseated from the course of his own life. He informed the station agent, flatly and without dramatics, that his regular run would require reassignment. Then he turned, coat unbuttoned despite the heat, and made his way to the office of Mayor J. Kenny Brown.

There, he delivered his intention with the same clarity one might use in submitting a schedule change: he was the man who had shot Colonel Parsons, and he was prepared to answer for it.

He asked for paper to send a telegram. He asked for something to eat. He asked—politely—to be placed under arrest.

Constable Brown obliged. No struggle ensued. No manacles were used.

By late afternoon, Goodman sat in the town lock-up, a structure more fit for drunks and gamblers than men accused of capital crimes. Word spread fast—not by newspapers just yet, but by the velocity of astonished mouths. Telegraph wires sang. The news reached Covington before the sun dipped behind the ridge.

County magistrate E. A. Snead arrived shortly before twilight. He found Goodman calm, upright, sitting on a wooden bench in shirtsleeves, gazing at nothing. The formal commitment was processed without fanfare. Witnesses later described the captain's demeanor as neither defiant nor contrite, but marked by a strange resignation—as though this chapter had long been authored, and he was simply reading it through.

No court date was announced, but all knew it would come swiftly. Justice, in a town still startled by its own stillness, did not wait long in those days. Not when blood had been spilled so plainly. Not when the name of a respected colonel lay on every tongue from Alleghany to Lexington.

In the week to come, lawyers would be summoned. Affidavits prepared. Defense and prosecution would marshal their arguments with precision befitting the gravity of the act. But in this first hour, as the lanterns dimmed across the inn and the smoke of morning still clung to its roofbeams, a different truth was felt: that in stepping forward to meet the law,

Goodman had not merely confessed to the killing—he had tethered himself to its aftermath, willingly and without disguise.

*****

On Wednesday, August 8, 1894, Covington's County courthouse awoke under a sweltering summer sun, its steps and corridors already lined with spectators drawn by the promise of spectacle and resolution. The charge before the court was dire: Captain William R. Goodman, long conductor for the Chesapeake & Ohio Railway, had been indicted by the grand jury just the previous Tuesday for the deliberate killing of Colonel Henry C. Parsons.

In the dozen weeks since the shooting at the Gladys Inn, rumor had transformed into narrative. Some claimed Goodman had been defending family honor; others argued the act was premeditated vengeance. Regardless, the matter had passed from muted conversations in Clifton Forge to public obsession in Covington—where every rumor begged verification under oath.

By mid-morning, the courtroom overflowed. Merchants in starched collars perched beside farmers in work-worn vests; women in summer gowns hushed their children. Even the air carried a tension unusual for a mountain town more accustomed to jury disputes over fences than mortal vendettas.

Goodman entered, flanked by deputies. His bearing was deliberate. The weight of months behind bars showed in pale skin and a steady tread, but his posture remained dignified.

The clerk read the indictment in measured formality: "Murder, with malice aforethought." The words rang clearly, suspending the room in collective stillness.

Then the moment arrived. Goodman rose. Voice controlled, gaze meeting the bench, he announced in calm, unwavering diction: *"Not guilty."*

And with that, the legal contest began.

The trial spanned eight days, presided over by Judge C. F. Moore. The Commonwealth, unsparing in tone, constructed a case of deliberate execution. Witnesses recounted Goodman's grip upon Parsons' sleeve, the silent escort from porch to parlor, and the grim finality of five gunshots discharged without visible provocation.

Supplementary materials—letters of anonymous origin and secondhand accounts—were permitted into evidence by the court, despite protest from the defense. These alluded to alleged indiscretions in Goodman's conduct—none rising to legal indictment, but sufficient, perhaps, to tarnish the moral lens through which the jury might view his actions.

The defense argued that Goodman, confronted by a threat to his person or family, had acted from the harrowing calculus of self-preservation. Yet, the image of a man fatally wounded by five deliberate shots weighed heavily on every mind in the courtroom.

When the jury retired, they were not away long. Their verdict—read before the evening glow—declared Goodman guilty of first-degree murder. Judge Moore pronounced an eighteen-year sentence to the state penitentiary. The decision felt final, punctuated by the collective sigh of a county convinced of righteous resolution.

Yet even then, beyond the echoes of the gavel, the seeds of appeal were planted. Duress over the admission of extrinsic character evidence constituted a judicial misstep—a legal error that soon compelled the Circuit Court of Alleghany County to order a new trial.

With Judge Moore stepping aside and one of Goodman's former attorneys elevated to the judiciary, the retrial was destined for Charlottesville, where neither defendant nor victim carried built-in advantage.

Thus, while Goodman left Covington under sentence, the verdict remained provisional—subject to the higher court's scrutiny, and to the promise of a fresh stage in a more impartial venue.

4

The People v. Goodman

By early spring of 1895, Charlottesville's court was prepared to receive what had already become one of the most scrutinized cases in the commonwealth. The courthouse was more modest than Covington's, its galleries quieter, the air less theatrical.

Here, the prosecution's arsenal was leaner—stripped of the inflammatory ephemera that had once drawn gasps from the gallery. The defense, by contrast, had been disciplined by the wounds of the first trial. It emerged neither triumphant nor defiant, but studied—its strategy sharpened by the errors it had endured. Their counsel did not aim to charm the court with oratory but to anchor the case in restraint.

It was against this more tempered backdrop that the proceedings commenced in earnest. The theater of accusation resumed—less grand, perhaps, but no less consequential.

As opening arguments began, the prosecution moved swiftly to frame a narrative of premeditation. The Commonwealth's attorney, a thin man with a clipped beard and a voice that held the sharpness of legal precision, stepped forward. His eyes rested not on the jury at first, but on Goodman himself.

"Gentlemen," he began, "this is not a case of impulse. This is not the flash of a quarrel turned tragic. This, I submit to you, is a *pattern*."

Decades before Clifton Forge would witness the fatal shot at the Gladys Inn, Captain William R. Goodman had already been tested by violence and found himself before a Virginia court.

It began unremarkably enough in a railroad yard near Staunton. Goodman and engineer Charles Porter had worked alongside one another for years, their tensions buried beneath duty and steam. But one afternoon, something ignited—perhaps a dispute over hours, perhaps a slight neither would forgive. In any case, Porter drew a knife. Goodman responded with calm ferocity, producing a concealed Derringer from his coat.

The sight of the firearm caused Porter to retreat, but only to rearm. Moments later, he returned, this time with a revolver and a grim resolve to settle the matter by other means. Goodman, ever alert to the geometry of threat, had already taken his stance.

"You're coming at me now, are you?" he is reported to have said—not as a taunt, but with the clarity of one who knows exactly how quickly the space between breath and bullet can vanish.

As he had anticipated, bullets tore the air almost instantly after that, cracking off stone and wood but striking no flesh. When their revolvers clicked dry, the fight turned savage. With nothing left to shoot, they began to beat one another with the butts of their pistols—swinging blindly, cursing through bloodied lips. Onlookers rushed toward them but dared not interfere.

At the height of it, Goodman wrestled free, raised the Derringer once more, and pressed it to the side of Porter's head. The barrel glinted. He pulled the trigger.

However, fate—or an unknown bystander—intervened. A hand struck his arm upward at the last second. The shot went wild, lodging harmlessly in a timber overhead.

The trial that followed was quiet compared to what lay ahead. The court deemed Goodman's actions a matter of self-defense, provoked by imminent threat. The verdict was acquittal, and for a time, the incident faded into the private annals of railway gossip and courtroom record books. However, the scars—both physical and reputational—remained.

"In that instance," the prosecutor concluded as the courtroom was brought back to the present moment. "Mr. Goodman was acquitted—deemed to have acted in self-defense. But gentlemen, I ask you: how many times must a man place a pistol against another's skull before we begin to question the measure of his restraint?"

He returned the document to the table with quiet finality.

"This trial is not about past grudges," he said. "It is about what happened on June 20th. But no event, no act of violence, stands entirely apart from the man who commits it. And this man's past, I submit, speaks volumes."

Silence fell for a beat too long before the judge gave a nod, subtle but sufficient, and proceedings resumed their course.

Goodman sat upright at the defense table, his expression unreadable, hands loosely folded before him as if in quiet command of himself. On either side of him were his attorneys—Mr. Beverly T. Crump, Mr. R. L. Parrish, and Mr. George Anderson—each man seasoned and reputed for their ability to manage a jury like a locomotive crew managed a throttle: with precision and caution.

Across the aisle, the Commonwealth's case was led by W. E. Allen and William E. Craig of Staunton, their papers ordered in stiff portfolios, their tone sharpened by the moral clarity they meant to assert. The man seated at the bench, Judge McLaughlin, barely thirty and newly appointed, bore the dual weight of law and novelty. His eyes scanned the courtroom with composure, betraying no hint of uncertainty, only a youthful sternness cultivated quickly on the circuit.

"Mr. Allen, you may call your first witness."

The prosecutor rose. "The Commonwealth calls J. Ed Martin."

Heads turned as the tall, slightly stooped figure of the hotel clerk emerged from the second row. Dressed plainly in a dark coat that seemed one size too large, Martin removed his hat with both hands as he crossed to the witness stand. He was sworn in with quiet formality, then seated.

Martin was not a man accustomed to public attention. His fingers fidgeted at the rim of his chair as he cleared his throat. The courtroom watched him with the kind of attentiveness that turns testimony into theater.

He began by identifying himself as the desk clerk at the Gladys Inn, employed there at the time of the incident. He spoke plainly, with the soft accent of the upper Valley, his words careful but not rehearsed.

"I knew both gentlemen," he said. "Captain Goodman had stayed with us before. Colonel Parsons was staying the night as usual, having arrived by train the evening prior."

He recounted the hour, the stillness of the inn in those early minutes after sunrise. He had been behind the registration desk when the voices first carried—low at first, then firm. He recalled hearing Goodman's sharp call: *"Come out here!"* It had drawn his attention at once.

"I went to the window to see what was happening," Martin continued, "and was in the act of raising the sash when the first report rang out."

He paused then, eyes drifting slightly to the wood floor of the witness box, as though searching it for the moment that had passed too quickly to fully register.

"I heard no more words," he added. "Only the shots—close together. Five, maybe more. I couldn't tell which man fired first."

Gasps rippled softly through the gallery. Martin's account, though sparse, had landed heavily.

When he stepped down, the next to take the stand was Henry Moody, the headwaiter at the Gladys Inn. A man of measured words and clear recollection, Moody's account added both proximity and immediacy to what had already been a chilling reconstruction.

He recalled seeing Captain Goodman in the dining room when a sound from the adjoining lobby caused him to glance toward the threshold. Goodman, turning toward the commotion, gestured in the direction of the figure beyond the doorway and asked Moody plainly: "Ain't that Colonel Parsons?" When Moody affirmed it was, Goodman's reply was curt—more a declaration than a question: "I've a mind to go out after him."

And when asked what business compelled such action, he replied that Parsons had written something against him—a letter that would not be left unchallenged. Nothing further was said. The Captain stepped out, retrieved his satchel from the rack, and moved through to the reading room.

Moments later, he returned, no longer carrying the satchel. His pace was brisk, his expression composed but set. Moody then watched as Goodman approached Parsons, extended a folded sheet of paper, and with one hand gripped the lapel of the Colonel's coat. "Here's this letter," he said. Then, sharply: "Come out to the front."

The two men passed through the front doors and out onto the porch. It was not long before they reappeared, but something had changed. Goodman's grip on Parsons had not slackened. Moody, standing just inside, watched as they crossed back into the lobby.

Then, without warning, Goodman reached with his free hand toward his side and drew a pistol. Parsons called out for Mr. White—the inn's manager—but the appeal was drowned almost instantly by the report of the first shot. Goodman continued to fire in rapid succession, each shot deliberate. His revolver was emptied in what seemed like mere seconds.

When pressed during cross-examination, Moody admitted he had not seen Colonel Parsons make any move to reach for a weapon—*or indeed for anything at all*. Captain Goodman, he noted, had been directly between him and the Colonel during the critical moments, obscuring his view. Nor could he testify to any exchange of words that may have taken place while the two men stood on the porch outside. Whatever passed between them in that brief interval, Moody confessed, had been lost to distance and the thick silence of foreboding.

In the days following the shooting, the prosecution had gathered additional testimonies from others who had encountered Goodman in the hours before the confrontation. These included rail employees and porters—men who had spoken casually with the conductor, not knowing they stood on the brink of an irrevocable event.

One such witness recounted that Goodman, while boarding the morning train at Natural Bridge, inquired whether Colonel Parsons was at home. The question had struck him as unremarkable at the time—one man seeking another, as travelers often do. Another testified that Goodman had made a similar inquiry at the inn itself, asking one of the staff whether Colonel Parsons was expected to arrive that morning.

Each question, when viewed in hindsight, took on the character of reconnaissance—small, deliberate steps in the lead-up to a fatal encounter.

To further illuminate the undercurrents of motive and premeditation, the Commonwealth called to the stand M. L. Akers, a clerk in the office of General Manager G. W. Stevens of the Chesapeake & Ohio Railway. He was not present at the shooting, nor even in Clifton Forge that week, but his testimony held weight of a different sort. He came bearing the trail of correspondence—official, dated, and damning.

Under questioning, Akers confirmed that in early June, a letter had been received at the Richmond office of the railroad. It was unsigned but composed on the personal stationery of Colonel Henry C. Parsons. Despite the absence of a signature, the content left little doubt as to its origin, and no objection had ever been raised as to its authenticity.

With deference to its sensitive nature, the letter was not read aloud in full, but Akers was permitted to outline its contents for the record. It spoke of alleged misconduct on Goodman's part— ranging from professional discourtesy to morally dubious behavior aboard the trains.

The tone, Akers said, was not merely accusatory but corrective. Parsons had written not as a private man aggrieved, but as a former officer and hotelier making what he believed to be a necessary report to company leadership.

The letter had passed from General Manager Stevens to Superintendent Doyle, and from there to Division Superintendent C. C. Walker, who, in accordance with protocol, brought it directly to Captain Goodman for reply. Goodman had submitted a written defense, though the details of that reply were not presented in court that morning.

The prosecution's case, once reliant on witness recollection, had now acquired the gravity of an administrative record.

There had been conflict.

As Akers stepped down, the courtroom momentarily stilled. The sequence was assembling itself—gesture by gesture, document by document. And though the defense had not yet begun its argument in full, the prosecution had laid its foundation.

5

Character Assassination

From the moment Captain Goodman entered his plea of *not guilty*, his counsel signaled a strategy that stood in sharp contrast to the prosecution's directness. While the Commonwealth had built its narrative around chronology and eyewitness recollection, the defense chose discretion. They withheld their most provocative piece of evidence—Goodman's reply to Colonel Parsons's letter—not out of oversight, but as a matter of design.

It was a deliberate silence, and one that drew quiet criticism from the gallery and observers. Why, some asked, did the defense not present the very grievance at the heart of the shooting? But Mr. Crump appeared to understand something others did not: timing in the courtroom was not unlike timing on the railroad. Too early a move, and the whole line was thrown out of sync.

So instead of launching with declarations or impassioned defenses, the first week was spent assembling a careful profile of the accused. One by one, men from the C&O—some

uniformed, some now retired—were called to the stand. Their recollections were plain, practical, and laced with the language of working men.

Captain Goodman, they testified, was no stranger to conflict. In eighteen years of rail service, he had enforced company regulations with an unwavering will. He had made enemies, yes—but not through violence. He was known more for his stern bearing and punctual reports than for any erratic temperament. His record was clean, his habits sober. Some described him as a "man of duty," others as "unbending," even "rough"—but never *dangerous*.

From the defense's side, this was not contradiction—it was scaffolding. They did not seek to disprove the shooting; they sought to recast the man who fired the shots.

It was in the latter half of that week, once the portrait of Goodman as a disciplined company man had been fixed in the minds of the jurors, that the defense made its calculated pivot.

"Your Honor," he began, rising with studied calm, "at this time, the defense would submit for the court's consideration a written reply—authored by the defendant and delivered into the hands of Mr. C. C. Walker on the twenty-eighth day of June."

There was a brief stir from the gallery. But Judge McLaughlin, seated high above in his walnut chair, gave a brief nod and lifted his palm.

"Counsel, approach the bench."

Mr. Crump and Mr. Allen rose in tandem and crossed the creaking floorboards to where the Judge leaned forward, his expression unreadable beneath his wire spectacles. The court stenographer followed close behind, pen poised.

In hushed tones, the judge spoke. "Is this the letter concerning Mr. Parsons's allegations to the railway company?"

Crump nodded. "It is, Your Honor. A direct rebuttal to the very document that—while unsigned—has colored this entire affair."

Allen interjected. "Your Honor, the Commonwealth objects to its admission at this late hour. The letter predates the trial by weeks and should have been entered in discovery. Its timing..."

Judge McLaughlin lifted a hand. "I am well aware of its timing, Mr. Allen. That is precisely why we are here."

He paused, considering both men in turn.

"This court does not take lightly the withholding of material so central to the matter of motive. And while the rules of this Commonwealth grant certain latitude in trial order, it must be made plain that delay is not license for surprise."

Then, after a moment's further reflection, he sat back and adjusted his cuffs.

"However, the document's relevance is evident. The jury will not be punished for what the law permits. The objection is overruled. The letter will be marked and entered as Defense Exhibit Twelve."

The clerk reached for the letter, recorded the entry into the court ledger, and passed it to the bailiff, who placed it with care into the evidence file.

Judge McLaughlin leaned back, then gave two deliberate raps of the gavel.

"This court will recess for two hours. Counsel may use the interval to prepare such procedural motions or accompanying testimony as they deem necessary. No further discussion of the exhibit shall occur until proceedings resume."

He rose from his chair and turned toward the side chamber, the long hem of his robe catching the corner of his desk as he passed. The bailiff called the court to recess, and the room slowly emptied, murmurs rippling just beneath the rules of decorum.

The jury, escorted out by the deputy, remained silent, unaware of the contents of the letter they would, in time, be called to weigh—but not yet. For now, it remained sealed. A hinge, waiting.

*****

At the stroke of the hour, the bailiff's voice rang out once more: "Court is now in session." A creak of pews and the shuffle of boots followed as jurors resumed their posts. Judge McLaughlin re-entered without remark, his robe settling heavily about his frame as he reclaimed the bench.

Mr. Crump rose slowly, hands clasped at the small of his back. He approached the lectern not as a man rushing to vindicate, but as one preparing to translate ink into character.

"Gentlemen of the jury," he began, "you have heard much over the past days about character—spoken through colleagues, questioned by rumor, and distorted by implication. Today, I ask you to hear the voice of the man himself."

He unfolded the letter slowly, the paper crackling faintly in the hush.

"This is a written appeal. A reply, composed in Richmond, not in anger, but in protest. Protest not against discipline or regulation, but against a pattern of maligning innuendo—unsigned allegations sent up the chain of command. This is the voice of a railroad man defending his name in the only proper way afforded to him: on paper, with his name at the bottom."

He opened it and read, his voice deliberate:

"It seems to be assumed... that the author of this libel is H. C. Parsons... I refrain from characterizing as it deserves the falseness of the attack made upon me by an enemy whose hostility I seem to have incurred solely by rigid adherence to my duty in the service of this company."

Crump paused, letting the gravity of that line settle.

"The statements in the unsigned communication are utterly false and without any foundation, except such as may be found in a malice that has no regard for the truth and justice."

He glanced briefly toward the jury and found no shift in their expressions. That was not what he had anticipated, still, he read on:

"I have not the least knowledge of who are the parties referred to... and I do not believe that complaint was ever made by any such persons..."

He turned a page.

"I have never been dismissed from the R & R road, and am not in the habit of boasting about anything. Any assistance that I

can render further in the matter, I will most cheerfully do, and will willingly stand any investigation should you deem such necessary."

Crump looked down at the desk before him, laid the letter gently beside his notes, and exhaled once before turning back to the jury.

"These are not the ravings of a violent man," he said. "They are the appeals of one accused without proof, his livelihood endangered by vague accounts and unnamed sources. Captain Goodman did not answer this affront with rage. He did not go to the press. He did not call witnesses of his own. He wrote. He waited. He asked to be heard."

Turning back to the jurors, he offered no plea, only this:

"This reply—this act of restraint—was handed in person. It was received, read, and shelved. No action was taken. No investigation followed. No reply was sent. The man you see before you today," he gestured briefly toward Goodman, seated at the defense table, "was given no hearing, no audience, no fair reckoning—only silence in return."

And with that, he stepped back to the defense table, sat down, and said nothing more. The letter, resting where he left it, had spoken its share. But the defense's moment at center did not linger untouched.

Rising with unhurried confidence, Mr. Allen adjusted his waistcoat and approached the well.

"If it please the court," he started, "the defense has furnished the jury with Captain Goodman's written reply to the allegations made against him. And indeed, its tone is civil, its construction sound. But let us not mistake composition for character."

He paced once before the jury rail, then came to a stop and folded his hands behind his back—a stance more professorial than prosecutorial.

"You have heard Mr. Crump describe the letter as an appeal for fairness, and perhaps in isolation, that is so. But we are not here to judge words alone. We are here to reckon with the hours that followed."

Allen turned toward Judge McLaughlin, then back to the jurors.

"Let the record show, and let it be plain: this letter was handed to Mr. Walker the morning of June the twenty-eighth— mere hours before the defendant armed himself, followed Colonel Parsons into the vestibule of a public inn, and fired upon him until the chambers of his revolver rang empty."

He paused, letting silence do the rest.

"What was submitted in writing may reflect a man's posture before authority," he concluded, "but it is his conduct under strain that tells the truth."

Allen let the last line hang in the stillness before resuming.

"Nor should we overlook," he said, stepping forward once more, "that this letter—elevated in its diction, tempered in its expression—was not followed by patience, nor by further petition. It was followed by inquiry."

He turned slightly, making eye contact with the row of jurors.

"Witnesses have testified that the accused was seen asking after Colonel Parsons that very morning—at the depot, at the inn, in the corridor where staff pass with linens and ledgers. He did not stumble upon the Colonel. He sought him."

A subtle murmur from the gallery was quelled with a tap of the bailiff's gavel.

Allen pressed on, his tone sharpening. "This was not outrage flaring in the moment. This was intent. Intent wrapped in civility, yes, but intent nonetheless. The very restraint that the defense offers you today as virtue—was the silence before action."

He turned, one hand now extended loosely, palm up.

"The law does not condemn a man for writing a letter. It does not convict on temperament or tone. But it does concern itself with deeds. And here, gentlemen and ladies, we have a sequence of them: inquiry, approach, confrontation, and finally—execution."

He let the last word stand, unadorned.

"In the final hours of June the twenty-eighth, Captain Goodman became more than a man offended. He became a man resolved. And it is that resolve—not the penmanship of his reply—that this court must consider."

6

The Most Damnable Charge

With motive no longer shrouded, the trial advanced into treacherous waters. The prosecution, having drawn a clear path to premeditation, now turned its sights to the particulars that had long stirred beneath the surface. Allegations once consigned to rumor were summoned forth, not for color, but for scrutiny.

As was the custom in trials of grave import, the most serious charge was taken up first—not for its salaciousness, but because the law demanded it be so.

"Your Honor, the Commonwealth now moves to address the third numbered allegation, as set forth in the letter submitted by the late Colonel Parsons. For this, we call Mr. J.E. Staples to the stand."

The name caused a stir among those familiar with the district. Staples worked the Springwood section, roughly five miles from Saltpetre Cave—the very locale where, according to Parsons's letter, Captain Goodman had once made improper overtures to a married woman.

Mr. Craig proceeded, "Mr. Staples, do you recall receiving letters from Captain Goodman in September of 1891 concerning an incident involving your wife?"

Mr. Staples affirmed, "I do, sir."

At this juncture, Mr. Parrish, interjected, "Objection, Your Honor. The letters in question were not disclosed during the initial discovery phase. Their sudden introduction is prejudicial to the defense."

"If I may, Your Honor—while Colonel Parsons's letter, which the defense itself has leaned upon, raised this very incident by name and place, we submit these documents not as new matter, but as corroboration. They were recovered from Mr. Staples's effects at our request after the trial had commenced, and their authenticity is not in question. We only now seek to admit what the defense has made unavoidable."

Judge McLaughlin glanced between them.

"Given the defense's choice to withhold their own material until this late juncture, it is only fitting that we now complete the record as it stands," Mr. Craig added.

After a brief deliberation, the judge ruled, "*The court will admit the letters into evidence.*"

The prosecution's small victory in securing the Staples letters did little to steady the rhythm of the day. What should have opened the way for testimony now gave rise to yet another spate of delay—petitions, rebuttals, quiet consultations at the bench, and long pauses as the judge reviewed precedents by lamplight. Each side, wary of yielding ground, treated every procedural motion as a battlefield in miniature.

In the jury box, the mood shifted perceptibly. The novelty of their civic duty had worn down beneath the slow press of repetition and interruption. And now, with day slipping toward its end, the court stood no closer to a decisive conclusion.

*****

The first letter, penned by Captain Goodman in September of 1891, denied improper contact with Mrs. Staples altogether. He admitted to speaking with her but described his inquiry as light in tone—asking, as he wrote, *"in a joking way,"* whether Springwood was good for fishing, and whether *"she could get up a party and go,"* under the impression that she was unmarried. He closed the letter demanding to know who had circulated such a falsehood and lamenting that his feelings had been *"wounded by so unfounded an accusation."*

The second letter, also dated that same month, bristled more plainly. It referred to an account relayed to Mr. Staples by a Mrs. and Miss Phelps, which Goodman denounced as *"a damned lie."* He wrote that he had once nearly put Miss Phelps off his train for lack of fare and suspected revenge. *"They do her no credit,"* he added, *"and worse—they injure your wife's name, who I consider a perfect lady."*

He ended by advising Staples to cut ties with the Phelps family and asserted that, had time allowed, he would have pursued both women under charges of slander.

Now that the context was introduced, Mr. Craig found the ground to build the rest of his case.

"Mr. Staples, you testified earlier that you were in receipt of two communications from the accused, dated September of '91.

May I ask—prior to those letters, had your wife received any correspondence, written or spoken, from Captain Goodman?"

Staples answered plainly, "No, sir. Not to her knowledge, nor mine."

"And she informed you of this herself?"

"She did. Said no letter ever reached her hands."

Craig lifted a paper from the desk and placed it back down again without comment, then looked squarely at the witness.

"Did your wife, of her own accord, bring to your attention any impropriety in Captain Goodman's behavior toward her?"

"She did, yes."

"How often?"

"Two or three times, over the course of some weeks."

Craig clasped his hands behind his back. "And what, precisely, did she allege?"

"She said Captain Goodman had made remarks to her—friendly, at first—but with implications, which turned more overt with time."

"And what did you do upon hearing this?" Craig inclined his head.

"I told her she ought not ride any train under his charge."

"No further questions."

With that, the prosecution yielded.

Mr. Parrish stood and approached the rail. His manner was less direct, more probing.

"Mr. Staples, you say your wife could read—was she literate in the usual sense?"

Before Staples could answer, Mr. Craig rose sharply from the prosecution's table.

"Objection, Your Honor," he called, his voice cutting through the hush. "Counsel is treading toward matters irrelevant to the core of the allegation. The witness's wife's education bears no material relevance to the truth of what was said or done."

Judge Moore, who had been following the exchange with attentive stillness, raised a hand and gestured for calm.

"Mr. Parrish," he said, "you will speak to the point."

Parrish responded evenly. "Your Honor, it is the defense's position that the credibility and reliability of the alleged report—and by extension, of those recounting it—rest in no small part upon the means by which it was conveyed. If the court is to consider claims delivered by letter or by word of mouth, it must also consider whether such communication could have been understood as claimed."

Judge McLaughlin gave a slow, deliberate nod. "Objection overruled."

He turned to Staples. "You may answer the question."

Staples shifted in his seat, his hands folded neatly in his lap as though clinging to a former composure.

"She could manage a few lines," he said, voice flat. "Enough to read a church notice or her name on a parcel. But she never kept a pen of her own. She'd have asked for help."

Parrish gave a nod, not of sympathy but recognition.

"So, to confirm, had Captain Goodman addressed anything directly to your wife in writing, she would not have been able to make full sense of it unaided?"

"She'd have come to me, or to the agent at the station—someone she trusted."

"Yet you state she received no such letter?"

"None, sir," Staples reinforced.

A murmur flickered at the back of the courtroom, quickly hushed by the bailiff's glance.

"You have mentioned two women—Mrs. Phelps and her daughter—as the ones who first brought this matter to your notice. Would you kindly state their relation to you?"

Staples adjusted in his chair, the wood creaking under his shifting weight. He clutched his hat in both hands, thumbs tracing slow, nervous circles around the brim. "They're kin, sir," he said, voice low and gruff, eyes downcast. "My sister and her girl."

"And how long had it been since you'd last seen them before this trial began?"

"Over a year. Might be nearer to two."

There was a pause. One of the jurors cleared his throat.

"What, precisely, did they report to you?"

"Said Captain Goodman had invited my wife on a fishing excursion," Staples hesitated. His hands stilled on the hat, then resumed their nervous movement. "Made it sound... improper."

Parrish walked a measured pace along the rail. "And prior to their telling, had you heard any such claims from your wife?"

"Not in so many words. She'd said Captain Goodman had spoken to her, but I reckoned it harmless at first."

"Did your wife ever claim that an invitation to travel had been extended?" Parrish asked, tone clipped, pressing now.

"Not directly. She said he'd mentioned Springwood and asked about the fishing there."

Parrish's eyebrows arched slightly, but he kept his expression neutral. "So, the core accusation—that Captain Goodman asked her to go off with him—was it based on what your wife told you, or on what your sister and niece alleged?"

A long beat passed.

"I suppose... both," Staples drew in a breath, slow and audible, then exhaled it through his nose. "I was stirred up at the time. Didn't know what to believe."

"Yet it was your wife's name that Captain Goodman felt compelled to defend in his letter."

"Aye," Staples admitted. "He said she was a lady. Said the Phelps were trying to cause trouble."

"Did he not also express," Parrish went on, "that he'd have them both charged with slander, had time and means allowed?"

Staples swallowed. "He did. But—"

Parrish's voice cut in sharply, the courtesy peeling away. "Mr. Staples—let me finish."

"So," he said slowly, turning back to face the witness, "to summarize, Mr. Staples: your wife did not receive a letter from Captain Goodman; the women who informed you were estranged relatives; and your accusations were conveyed to Goodman in writing, to which he responded promptly— denying the charge, defending your wife's name, and casting doubt upon the accusers?"

Staples nodded, almost imperceptibly at first, then with more conviction.

Parrish inclined his head. "That will be all, your honor."

*****

After a brief recess, the court was back in session.

Mr. Parrish rose once more, this time with a faint air of calculation, as though laying a final card on the table whose value was not immediately evident.

"Your Honor, the defense now calls Miss Adelaide Phelps."

There was a faint ripple in the gallery—whispers stifled by stern glances. The name had been invoked often enough to acquire its own gravity, and now the bearer of it stepped forward, her youth somewhat obscured by the severity of her dress. Clad in plain serge with a tightly drawn waist, Miss Phelps climbed the witness stand with a kind of quiet resolve, her gloves removed and tucked into a reticule held fast against her side.

Once sworn, she settled into the chair, hands resting primly in her lap.

Parrish's tone was courteous but spare. "Miss Phelps, for the benefit of the court, would you state your relation to Mr. J.E. Staples?"

"He is my uncle, sir."

"And the woman seated beside you?"

"My mother, Eugenia."

Parrish nodded slightly, as if to confirm details already known.

"Miss Phelps, you've heard reference in this court to a report delivered by you and your mother to Mr. Staples, concerning an interaction between Captain Goodman and his wife. Do you recall the date?"

"It was the ninth of September 1891."

"And what, precisely, did you witness?"

She drew a breath. "We were passing through the depot square at Springwood when we saw Mrs. Staples on the platform. Captain Goodman had approached her. He stood uncommonly close. He laughed, then reached his hand toward the neckline of her bodice. I cannot say he touched her, but his fingers made some gesture—light, perhaps—but overly familiar."

Parrish held his posture, neither turning from the jury nor advancing further toward the witness box. His voice remained mild, but it carried a new undertone—less accommodating, more precise.

"And what was your impression of the exchange?"

"That it was not fitting," she said firmly. "Not between a gentleman and a married woman."

"Did you communicate this impression to Mr. Staples?"

"We did. Within the week."

"Did you assign blame to his wife?"

"No, sir. We said the captain's conduct was unseemly. Not hers."

Parrish gave a shallow nod, as if content, then paused—as though about to let her down gently from the stand. But then, with the same tone he might have used to inquire about the weather, he added:

"And had you, Miss Phelps," he inquired mildly, "ever made the acquaintance of Captain Goodman prior to that day at the Springwood depot?"

A hesitation, slight but perceptible, passed across her features.

"I had seen him, sir," she said at last. "On the train."

"Only seen him?"

"Yes."

Parrish tilted his head. "Never exchanged words?"

She hesitated.

"In fact," he continued gently, "had he not, at one point the previous year, asked that you be removed from the train for lack of fare?"

The hush that fell was sudden and complete. A faint tremor passed through her hands, which she folded tighter in her lap. "He did," she admitted.

"And was that expulsion carried out?"

"No," she said. "A family friend paid my fare."

Parrish's voice, while never raised, carried an unmistakable weight now, measured and exacting. "And did you feel that Captain Goodman had treated you unfairly in the moment?"

She glanced toward her mother, as though for assurance, but none was offered.

"It was uncalled for," she said suddenly, the words more forceful than intended. "I was not trying to ride unlawfully—I simply hadn't the coin at hand."

Her voice had risen—not quite to defiance, but audibly enough to ripple through the stillness of the chamber.

Parrish paused, then spoke with deliberate calm. "So, to clarify—you regarded the captain's decision as excessive?"

"I did," she replied, her cheeks mottling with color now. "It was needlessly harsh."

"And would you say that impression remained with you?"

When, for a few seconds, no response was forthcoming, Parrish pushed on. "Miss Phelps, we do not impugn your sincerity. But would it be fair to say that, by the time you observed his exchange with Mrs. Staples at the Springwood depot, your impression of Captain Goodman had already been shaped—at least in part—by the earlier fare dispute?"

Miss Phelps's lips parted as though to reply, but then closed again. When she finally spoke, her tone had altered.

"I know what I saw," she said, voice rising beyond its former decorum. "You may twist it how you like, sir, but I was there. My mother was there. That man reached toward another man's wife with a look in his eye that no decent woman would mistake."

There was a stir in the gallery.

Parrish remained still, only the slightest tilt of his head betraying any response.

"I did not imagine it," she continued, more loudly now. "Whatever happened on that train, it has no bearing here. This—*this*—was something else. And if you think you can embarrass me into silence, you'll not succeed."

Her voice had risen to the point that the judge inclined slightly forward. One of the court officers shifted in place, readying himself.

Parrish waited—cool, composed, letting the fury burn itself open.

"No one has sought to embarrass you, Miss Phelps," he said at last, evenly. "But the court must consider not only what was seen, but who was seeing it—and with what history."

She leaned forward as if to retort again, but the judge's voice intervened—low but definitive.

"That will do."

The damage had been done.

The judge turned toward the prosecution. "Mr. Craig?"

Craig conferred momentarily with his clerk, then stood without rising. "The Commonwealth has no questions for the witness."

"You may step down, Miss Phelps," said the judge, his voice even.

*****

The defense having yielded, and with the hour pressing toward the warmer end of the afternoon, the Commonwealth called its next and most anticipated witness.

"Mrs. Lucinda Staples."

Mr. Craig approached slowly, his tone respectful but firm.

"Mrs. Staples," he began, "you have heard testimony referring to certain remarks made to you by the accused—Captain Henry Goodman. Would you please recount, in your own words, the nature of those remarks?"

"He was forward," she said plainly. "Too forward for a man I scarcely knew. It was not once, but each time I rode the train, if he were on it. He would speak to me—sometimes jesting, sometimes flirtatious—though he knew I was married."

"And how did that make you feel?"

"I was insulted," she said, with more steel now in her voice. "I am a married woman, and it was not his place to speak to me as if I were something else."

190

Mr. Craig inclined his head. "Can you recall any specific remarks?"

Her hands tightened around her reticule.

"One day, he said he knew if I would go along and bait his hook, he would 'catch a big fish.' I thought it coarse and unbecoming." Mrs. Staples continued. "He said I was 'too fine a looking lady to be that old man's wife.' He meant my husband."

"And did he propose any course of action?"

"Yes," she said, her voice flattening with quiet distaste. "He told me he had money enough and would take me to Richmond. Said he'd rent a room, and I could bring any of my lady friends. Told me to tell my husband I was going to visit my brother, who lives near Lynchburg, and then I could go on with him."

"Did he ever suggest how he might convey this plan to you?"

"He said he would toss a note onto the porch as the train passed. He knew our house stood right along the tracks. He said he expected me to be waiting in the doorway."

"Was such a note ever delivered?"

She gave a single nod. "He came by the next day with the note in his hand. But I was in the parlor, and Kate Phelps was at the door. He didn't throw it."

Mr. Craig's eyes now lifted to the panel, meeting not each man but the idea of their collective conscience.

"This was not the idle play of a conductor exchanging words with a passenger. These were repeated overtures, sharpened by boldness, dressed in jest, and anchored in deceit. The accused did not merely remark upon her appearance—he invited her to abscond, to deceive her husband, to cross both miles and moral bounds under cover of false errand."

He gestured—not broadly, but briefly—with his left hand.

"We need not accuse him of success. The law is not reserved for what is carried out, but what is attempted with will. The defendant sought not merely the attention of a married woman, but her complicity. And when that failed, he left a wake of impropriety and insult too plain to ignore."

At that, Mr. Craig said no more, but returned to his seat.

Next, Mr. Parrish approached the witness stand with an air of tempered gravity. "Madam," he said, his voice almost pastoral in its softness, "you've made grave assertions under oath, and I do not doubt you believe them true."

Mrs. Staples gave no reply but folded her gloved hands more tightly in her lap.

Parrish took a measured pause before continuing. "And yet I must ask, if these overtures from Captain Goodman were so egregious, so offensive to your dignity as a wife and woman— why, then, did you continue to ride under his charge?"

"I had need to travel," she replied curtly. "My mother was ailing, and the train was the only way."

"Certainly. But need alone does not preclude discretion. Did you not once lodge a formal complaint? Or speak to another conductor?"

She hesitated. "No, sir."

"Not even when he said he would hurl a note upon your porch?"

"I told my husband," she said, her tone stiffening.

"Yes, you have said as much. And yet, when the train passed—when the note was said to be in hand—you were not away from sight, nor secluded in your room, but seated in the parlor, visible from the platform."

"I was at home," she snapped. "Am I to flee my own sitting room?"

Parrish bowed his head slightly, letting the sharpness of her reply speak for itself.

"One last matter, madam," he said, almost gently now. "You described an incident—when the captain assisted you from the train and, in doing so, 'scratched your hand' and looked at you in a manner you found objectionable. Did he say anything untoward?"

"No."

"Did he restrain you in any way?"

"No."

"Then the insult resided solely in the way he... looked?"

Mrs. Staples hesitated, then nodded. "He held on too long."

"And when he held on—too long, as you say—how long, madam? A moment? A breath's delay? Or long enough to draw comment from those beside you?"

"I beg your pardon, sir," she said, her brow furrowed. "But I don't understand—what do you mean by that?"

"Did you tell your husband about that plan before or after your sister-in-law and her daughter had already spoken with him?"

Mrs. Staples blinked. "I don't recall exactly."

"But to your knowledge, had your husband heard of the fishing party or the note before your relatives visited?"

"I—he may not have," she said. "But I know I told him."

"When?"

She looked toward the back of the room, as if searching for a clock that might rescue her.

"I can't say exactly."

"Mrs. Staples," Parrish said gently, "I do not question your memory in matters of feeling. But in matters of fact—timing, sequence—those are the measures by which this court must judge. So I ask again: did your husband learn of these invitations from you directly, or did he first hear them from his sister?"

Mrs. Staples's eyes narrowed, and for a moment she seemed to press forward in her chair, as though the impulse to correct or rebuke had overwhelmed her restraint. But she did not speak.

Instead, her silence—brimming with something unreadable—seemed to say more than her testimony had moments earlier. It hung there, brittle and unresolved, as Mr. Parrish slowly turned from her and addressed the bench.

"No further questions, Your Honor."

The precise measure of truth contained within her account could not be ascertained with finality. What did emerge—

quietly but unmistakably—was the erosion of credibility, not merely hers, but that of her husband and their kin alike. Whatever weight their words might once have carried was, by degrees, diminished.

7

The Threshold of Doubt

Commonwealth, sensing the shifting tide, did not relinquish the field without resistance. With its principal edifice fractured, the prosecution turned now to lesser stones—seeking, if not to restore the full weight of its case, then at least to seed doubt within the minds of the jury.

To this end, Mr. Craig requested the introduction of additional materials—correspondences and private accounts—that, though lacking direct indictment, aimed to suggest a pattern unbecoming of a man entrusted with public charge.

The intention was plain: to fortify character as circumstantial proof, and to impress upon the jury that while one testimony may falter, the aggregate of impropriety could not be wholly imagined.

The first among these supplementary exhibits was a letter—unsigned, but introduced with quiet solemnity as having passed through the office of the Railway Superintendent, with its envelope postmarked from a town near Lynchburg. Its language was unadorned, almost apologetic, but its contents spoke to unease.

The writer, identifying himself only as a "passenger of several years' acquaintance with the route," claimed to have observed Conductor Goodman "escort a woman into the ladies' closet during an afternoon run between Richmond and Lynchburg." The tone of the letter was cautious—its author expressed no wish to be named or involved—but made clear that the action "did not appear consistent with professional decorum."

The memorandum offered little more than that. There was no sworn affidavit, no physical description of the woman, and the alleged informant had expressly declined to make a formal statement. Still, the prosecution pressed the point: that the sheer peculiarity of the action, paired with its unsuitability aboard a public train, rendered it "worthy of judicial notice."

Mr. Parrish, for the defense, made no immediate objection, but his posture—a slight lean back and a faint narrowing of the eyes—signaled his readiness.

The second document was more pointed, though no less fragile in its evidentiary spine. It recorded the recollection of one Mr. Talcott, a bartender who had reportedly served aboard the same line in the summer of '91.

According to the note, Mr. Talcott *did witness what he took to be an improper familiarity* between the conductor and a female passenger, though the account lacked date, context, and specificity. Worse still, the bartender was no longer in Virginia, having removed to Cincinnati the previous autumn, and no deposition had been taken.

What lent the charge any vitality at all was the timing: the incident was said to have occurred within days of the Richmond–Lynchburg journey noted in the first memorandum. Mr. Craig sought to portray it as circumstantial corroboration—that two men, unknown to each other, had described similarly disquieting behavior in the same general window of time. Whether the jury would find the symmetry compelling remained uncertain.

The third was of a different order altogether: a report passed along by a domestic servant in the Holt household, who relayed that a young colored girl at Maiden's Adventure Station had boasted of being *"taken on"* by Captain Goodman for an overnight ride to Clifton Forge—ostensibly for his pleasure. The claim, unsworn and rooted in tavern chatter, bore all the marks of scandal, but none of legal shape.

Mr. Craig, for his part, did not attempt a rhetorical flourish. He placed the documents into the record, offered a summary of each with due solemnity, and stood aside.

Parrish, however, rose slowly.

"My learned colleague," he began, turning not to the court but to the jury, "has offered you fragments—reports without names, events without dates, allegations without authors. He has asked that you infer from silence what no one dares to assert aloud."

He took a measured breath.

"If this trial is to serve as a beacon of public justice and not descend into the fever of social suspicion, let us remember the principle that must guide all such deliberation: that a man cannot be condemned for the murmurs of a railway corridor, nor for the indistinct remembrances of men no longer within the reach of summons."

He turned slightly, glancing toward the exhibit table where the folded pages sat inert under their ribbon.

"It is not enough to suggest that Captain Goodman may have acted without grace. That is not the standard. It is not enough to present these papers and hope their ink will bleed into character. That is not the law."

The jury—whose bearing had earlier sagged beneath the strain of Mrs. Staples's halting and uncertain testimony—now straightened, as if called to attention not by conviction but by duty. The court required as much. And so too, it seemed, did Parrish—whose very posture implied that the expectations of the Republic itself hung upon their compliance.

It was a tenuous restoration of order, but one sufficient for the prosecution's next maneuver—a return to the place where its case had once found its footing. That moment—the fatal morning at the Gladys Inn—was where all remaining strength of the prosecution must now reside.

Thus, in accordance with both procedural latitude and strategic necessity, Mr. Craig submitted a modest but calculated petition: that two previously examined witnesses—Mr. J. Ed Martin and Mr. Henry Moody—be recalled for limited re-examination. His aim was to cast a clearer frame around prior testimony now rendered pivotal by the shifting tenor of the case.

The presiding judge assented with a wordless gesture, and the bailiff, with mechanical formality, summoned the first of the two.

Mr. Moody reappeared with a visible burden, as though summoned less to speak than to account for having spoken already. The courtroom, sensing the stakes of redundancy, shifted in its benches. Yet even in repetition, there are gradations; the law, like scripture, allowed a passage to bear new meaning in light of later chapters.

Mr. Craig approached now, leaning upon the slow grind of accumulation.

"Mr. Moody," he began, his voice tempered but firm, "prior to the discharge of the weapon, you observed both men enter and exit the adjoining room—correct?"

"I did."

"Would you describe his expression—his manner—as composed? Agitated? Impulsive?" Craig narrowed his eyes.

Moody hesitated. "Not agitated. Determined, perhaps."

"And then you mentioned they went outside. How long were they absent from view?"

"Perhaps two minutes. No more."

Craig paused, letting the phrasing hang. "And upon their return—was there any discernible alteration in their manner?"

"There was," Moody nodded faintly. "Goodman's grip had visibly tightened. Colonel Parsons no longer moved of his own accord, but rather as though being conducted—his bearing stiff, unyielding."

"Did you witness Colonel Parsons offer resistance? A raised hand, a sudden movement, a reach for a weapon?" Craig inclined his head, his expression austere.

"No, sir. None that I perceived. He called out—for Mr. White, the innkeeper—but the words had scarcely escaped him when the first report echoed through the room."

Moody's voice dropped a register, its gentleness replaced by a steadier resolve. "Then let the record reflect, Mr. Moody: you perceived no provocation—verbal or physical—that would justify the force used?"

"That is correct."

The purpose had been fulfilled.

And yet, it was not without fissures—those tiny, judicial fault lines which the defense surely knew would soon be pried open.

"Mr. Moody..." Parrish clasped his hands and regarded the worn-down witness with a surgical stillness, "You say you did not hear threats, nor see a weapon until the moment it was drawn. But you also testified that you could not hear what passed between the men when they stepped onto the porch."

"That is true."

"So, while you cannot confirm that Captain Goodman issued threats, neither can you say he did not?"

Moody gave a single, cautious nod.

"May I also ask you to recall—where exactly were you positioned in the lobby when the men returned from the porch?"

"Near the vestibule," Moody replied. "Just inside the main entry."

"Facing the front doors?"

"Partly. I was turned—like so," he gestured vaguely, "not square on."

Parrish inclined his head. "So, when you say you saw Mr. Goodman draw a pistol, you observed this from the side."

"Yes, sir."

"And at that angle, could you see Colonel Parsons's right hand?"

A pause. Moody frowned slightly. "Not clearly. His back was toward me then."

"Ah." Parrish stepped closer, as if to seal that recognition in the jurors' minds. "So, when you testified that Colonel Parsons did not have a weapon in hand, that was not because you saw an empty hand, but rather because his hands were not plainly visible to you at all."

"I suppose that is true," Moody was unsure of the direction in which this cross-examination was headed.

"Which means," Parrish concluded, stepping away, "that no man in this courtroom, not even you, can say whether my client fired in aggression, or in fear for his life."

A subtle ripple moved through the court, but no answer ever came forth.

A faint corrugation settled on Mr. Craig's brow. For a moment, he seemed to study the edge of the lectern as though some fresh angle might present itself there. Then, with composure regathered, he raised his voice—not in triumph, but with the precision of a man unwilling to relinquish his case to silence.

He turned to the bench and requested, with studied neutrality, that Mr. J. Ed Martin be recalled.

Mr. Craig inclined his chin. "Mr. Martin," he began, his diction clipped and tempered, "you testified previously that you were manning the front desk at the Gladys Inn on the morning of the incident?"

"Yes, sir. I was tallying the lodgers' accounts."

Craig clasped his hands before him, his posture rigid. "When Captain Goodman and Colonel Parsons re-entered from the porch, did you—at any point—observe them exchange words?"

"No, sir. Not a word passed between them that I could hear. It was a... tense silence, if I may call it that."

"Tense, how so?" Craig's brows knit faintly.

"The Captain's hold did not loosen—his hand fast upon the Colonel's sleeve. The Colonel averted his gaze. To my eye, he was not walking beside him, but being delivered—like a parcel, not a man."

"Did you observe any signs of resistance?"

Martin inhaled slowly. "No overt struggle. But it was clear— the Colonel was not proceeding of his own will."

"And did you see any indication that Colonel Parsons made a sudden move? A gesture suggesting aggression? A reach, perhaps, toward his coat or belt?"

Martin frowned slightly, summoning the moment from memory. "None that I recall."

"And at what precise moment did the firearm appear?"

Martin paused. "Just as they passed beneath the transom. Goodman stopped abruptly, turned somewhat, and reached across his own body."

Craig let the silence bloom before stepping back.

"No further questions at this time."

As he retreated to his table, the prosecutor's face was carefully composed, but something in his shoulders betrayed the labor it took to maintain that stillness. He did not sit.

"Mr. Martin," Parrish approached with neither bluster nor haste, "you've rendered a careful account—one which, I do not doubt, you have sought to convey with honesty. But may I trouble you for the order in which events impressed themselves upon your senses?"

Martin turned slightly toward him. "Yes, sir, if I can."

"Good. You testified that Captain Goodman halted beneath the transom, turned, and then—without exchange—drew his weapon. Do you recall your precise words?"

"I said he reached across his own body."

Parrish nodded. "Yes. But did you see the hand move first— or did you hear the first discharge before fully registering that he had drawn?"

"I... I saw him move. I believe I saw the motion first." Martin furrowed his brow.

"You believe, or you are certain?" Parrish's voice bore no edge—only the weight of precision.

"I am fairly certain."

Parrish took a small step forward, the hem of his coat sweeping just above the boards. "And in the interval between the gesture and the gun's report—did you have the time to look upon Colonel Parsons's face? His hands? His bearing?"

"No, I don't believe I did. It happened rather... all at once."

"Indeed," Parrish said quietly. "A man startled by gunfire often finds his memory compresses time—conflates what led to the act with the act itself."

Martin said nothing.

Parrish turned slightly, addressing not the bench, nor the jury, but the room at large. "Ladies and gentlemen, the witness has told us of what he believes he saw—but belief is not the coin of judgment. If his memory folds action into aftermath, we cannot weigh its parts as if they were distinct."

What had been presumed to be an open-and-shut affair—a public execution in all but name—now teetered on the threshold of reasonable doubt. Not because the event itself had changed, but because the reading of it had—sliced finer, interrogated deeper, and burdened with the gravity of judicial responsibility.

Captain Goodman, who had sat through the morning's proceedings with a military composure—chin forward, eyes level—tilted his head slightly then, in triumph. And the jury—those twelve citizens pulled from the mercantile, the fields, the workshops of the county—did not look at him as they had before. They looked longer now, as if to re-examine not merely what he had done, but what they had assumed.

*****

As dusk loosened its grip on the courtroom, twelve citizens retreated to the deliberation chamber, the door closing behind them like the final chord of a requiem. There, they faced not simply witness accounts, but the yawning uncertainty left in their wake.

Discussion advanced in stages. First, on the nature of perception: how a startled observer might misremember angle, distance, or intention. Second, on motive: whether Goodman truly believed himself under threat, or acted in haste born of malice. Third, on character citations: documents suggesting impropriety now revealed as anecdotal whispers, without legal form or direct bearing.

Alignments began to harden not along lines of ideology, but of interpretive threshold. A few held that whatever flaws remained in the prosecution's case, the act itself—five shots fired at close range—carried its own indictment. They returned again and again to the silence between Goodman and Parsons, to the manner in which the captain escorted the colonel back inside, not as a man reconciled to peace, but as one bracing for rupture.

Others, more circumspect, urged caution. They reminded the room that neither Moody nor Martin had seen Parsons' hands clearly, nor could they account for his final movements with precision. For all they knew, it could be an act of self-defense. A gesture unseen was not proof of its absence, and what the law demanded was not supposition, but clarity.

Over time, fatigue lent its own honesty. Postures relaxed. The ledger of argument grew thinner. The moral weight of the act remained, but the procedural scaffolding beneath it had begun to falter.

When they rose at last—each man folding his notes with quiet deliberation—there was no thunderclap, no breathless revelation. Only the solemn understanding that the verdict, whatever its implications, was not a measure of the soul, but of the statute. The threshold had not been met. Doubt, silent and durable, had done its work.

Therefore, Captain Thomas A. Goodman was found to be *'Not Guilty.'*

8

What Conscience Could Not Acquit

At the Henry Parsons homestead, no weeping met the news. There was only a kind of stillness—neither reverent nor stunned, but stilled in the way a house becomes when mourning has outlasted outrage.

Nellie Loomis Parsons, once known for her quiet elegance and fondness for society calls, had grown hollow-eyed in the months since her husband's killing. Her nerves, already frayed by years of intermittent illness, had not withstood the glare of public scrutiny. She had refused to attend the trials in Covington or Charlottesville. The details, when read aloud by her daughter Gretchen, seemed to strike not as new injuries but as the cruel finishing of old ones.

Gretchen, who had steadied herself for such an outcome, nevertheless felt the ground shift beneath her. She read the dispatch again, this time silently, her eyes lingering on each phrase, as though careful parsing might reveal some flaw in its verdict, some misprint that would restore the world to its rightful axis. But the ink held fast. Across the room, Maud stood at the window, fingers idly grazing the lace curtain's edge. Outside, the garden lay untended, its spring shoots encumbered by last year's dead stalks.

Henry had once tilled it himself, early each April, coat off, collar unbuttoned, hands dark with soil. She remembered him waving once to a passerby with his trowel—unaware, perhaps, of how easily men might mistake uprightness for arrogance. Now that same soil bore no seed, and no harvest would come of it.

Yet it was not only the garden that lay fallow.

News of Goodman's acquittal, when it reached the broader Commonwealth, stirred no such quietude. Where the Parsons home fell into subdued withdrawal, the rest of Virginia erupted into disquiet. From Alexandria to Danville, Norfolk to Pulaski, editorials bloomed like ragged blooms of dissent—sharp, angry, incredulous.

The press did not temper its judgment. Many called the verdict a miscarriage, a judicial farce. If a man could summon another from safety, draw him aside, fire upon him five times without warning—and walk free by invoking imagined peril— then the very bedrock of justice was cracked, if not broken.

There was more than morality at stake. Editorials warned that the decision endangered the state's reputation, particularly in the eyes of Northern capital.

With railroads expanding and industrial speculation rising, the South, and Virginia especially, had become a site of economic reinvestment. But what investor would trust his stake to a place where violence could be excused by sentiment and honor turned against reason? If justice could be gamed by performance—by gesture and innuendo—then the Commonwealth risked appearing not merely antiquated, but lawless.

Yet not all voices aligned. Some papers, particularly those wary of northern condescension, defended the jury's decision. They cautioned against public vilification of twelve men sworn to weigh evidence, not appease outrage.

It was not justice, they said, that had failed, but public understanding of its quiet burdens. The court, after all, had admitted what it had—facts, testimony, the tenor of threat— and left the rest to deliberation. If the result displeased, it was the law's own complexity, not corruption, that bore the blame.

Yet even as opinion pieces jostled for primacy in the public square, another current began to flow—less visible, but no less telling.

Beyond the inked broadsheets and rhetorical postures, there unfolded a quieter, more personal correspondence: a tide of letters, notes, and missives that made their way not to editors' desks, but to the grieving home on the edge of Lexington.

These were not the pronouncements of political organs or business journals, but the considered offerings of townspeople, distant relatives, former colleagues, and even strangers. Their tone varied—some measured, others fervent—but the message remained constant: that the acquittal had left behind a residue of sorrow and dismay not confined to the courtroom walls. They did not presume to override the jury's verdict, but neither did they mistake it for vindication.

Among the many letters that reached the Parsons household in the weeks to come, one stood apart—not for its eloquence, but for its unmistakable sincerity. Postmarked from Richmond on the first of April, the note arrived folded in coarse paper, its script uneven but deliberate.

"Dear Madam,

No doubt you may be somewhat surprised at receiving this communication from one whom you have never seen and may never see in this world, but after I have explained myself, I hope you will pardon me for taking this liberty of addressing you.

I noticed in yesterday's paper that you had made the statement that you did not intend to leave old Virginia on account of the unjust verdict. The Richmond papers have had very little—if anything—to say about it."

Nellie Parsons had chosen to remain in Virginia, despite the acquittal's bitter sting. She would not uproot the legacy her husband had spent a lifetime cultivating—not the land he had managed, nor the civic duties he had shouldered in quiet earnest. To leave now, in the wake of scandal and injustice, would be to abandon the memory of his integrity to rumor and misinterpretation.

Henry Parsons had not merely belonged to the soil of Virginia; he had invested himself in its betterment. In school boards, veterans' gatherings, and town committees, he had stood—firm yet unassuming—as a figure of stability in a region still mending from the fractures of war. His death, brutal and unredressed, had threatened to unravel that steadiness. But Nellie understood that to relinquish their place in the community would only compound the rupture.

And so, she stayed.

The decision was not born of comfort or pride, but of duty—to her daughters, to memory, and to the belief that truth, however obscured by courts and headlines, must still be honored in the living.

That strangers like the Richmond correspondent understood this, even in part, lent a faint but undeniable sense of fellowship.

"I expressed my opinion pretty freely on the subject and sent it to some of our daily papers, and they refused to publish it. I don't know the reason, unless they were afraid of offending someone. They returned it to me and gave me as their excuse for not publishing it that they had expressed their disapproval of the verdict previously, and thought it unnecessary to say any more about it.

But I don't think enough has been said in condemning Goodman for his dastardly crime. He ought to have the mark of Cain upon him and be ostracized by every right-thinking man and of the unjust verdict that had been given in the Goodman trial, as it had formerly been reported that you would do."

His choice of words revealed not only a moral revulsion, but a personal investment in the very idea of justice as a shared civic trust. This was not the language of idle commentary. It came from a man wounded, in his own way, by the implications of the verdict: that honor could be twisted into license, and that violence cloaked in sentiment might find legal refuge.

"I am glad that you are not going to leave the old state, I believe you have the sympathy of a large majority of the best people in the state, in your recent troubles, and it is as you said the twelve men who brought in the verdict in Charlottesville and those who

shouted and rejoiced over it do not represent the sentiments of the people of Virginia, but as you say, they are but the dross that comes from the pure metal, while the papers all over the country have been condemning."

My punctuation and spelling is not all correct but I hope you may be able to make it out, as you may wish to know something of the writer. I will just say that I am 29 years of age and have a wife and two little boys, and am a born Virginian, again expressing to you and your daughters my heartfelt sympathy for you in this sad calamity and asking your pardon for addressing you.

I am yours very truly, M. G. Mason"

Staying, then, had not simply been a refusal to yield to fear or humiliation—it was, as letters like Mason's made plain, a return to the living heart of a community still capable of moral discernment. And in that, there was something rarer than comfort. There was credibility.

Even the Commonwealth's own attorney, having fulfilled his public charge, took the uncommon step of writing privately to the Parsons household. His letter, delivered with discretion in the weeks following the verdict, arrived not as a procedural courtesy, but as a personal offering—a gesture that quietly acknowledged the deeper costs of the case, beyond the reach of law.

"Supplemented by that of the multitudes of members of secret organizations to which the accused belonged—was brought to bear, and the very air of the court house was charged with this death-lust. The fact is, that before I addressed the jury in conclusion, they had already reached the decision to acquit, and no reason or

eloquence that could be used to the contrary, was potent to induce them to reverse a conclusion already reached and settled.

You and your stricken family have this to console you—that a great host in the best and most conservative circles in Virginia sympathize with you deeply, and the great heart of the outraged state beats in touch with you and is drawn closer to you and the memory of your lamented husband.

Both my wife and myself are grateful to you for lending "The Reader" and other poems.

Kate has read them with the greatest interest and pleasure— and realizes how learned and gifted the author must have been— who was so rudely smitten down in the flower and bloom of his life.

Of the mere glimpses which we caught of you & your lovely daughters, we have drawn very near to all of you—and we hope that at some convenient season in future, we may have the pleasure and privilege of entertaining you & them at our house.

Please give to Mrs. Grafton and Miss Maud—from my wife & daughter & myself—our sympathetic & affectionate regards; and to Mr. Grafton, remember me most cordially—and believe me,

Most Sincerely Your, Friend."

Though his words reaffirmed what had been stated in court and repeated in public—namely, that the tide had turned long before summations were made—it also revealed something more private: a personal stake in the sorrow. The Commonwealth's attorney, though seasoned in courtroom procedure and well-acquainted with the cynicism of trial outcomes, did not write merely to console.

That he mentioned the poems at all signaled the extent to which he had been moved—not simply as an officer of the court, but as a man compelled by the dignity with which the family had borne their grief. He had, by his own admission, been stirred by Henry Parsons's moral stature, the kind rarely spoken of without ceremony and yet deeply felt by those who witnessed it. It was that character—quiet, immovable, and exacting—that had impressed itself upon him, and that, perhaps, made the trial's outcome harder to swallow.

9

The Legacy Remains

"There have been several different owners of the bridge since Colonel Parsons, but none have operated it as effectively as the Colonel."

Time advanced with the discretion of moss over stone—unbidden, unceremonious. The structure on the south road, its timbers grayed, had settled more deeply into the land, as if drawn downward by memory itself. Iron darkened to rusted ochre, the bolts smooth to the touch. But it was not the bridge that held the town's regard, not precisely. It was the man that gave the structure meaning.

Like many of his generation, Colonel Henry Parsons returned to find the land changed, frayed by loss and suspicion. But where others fell to inertia or grievance, he set to work.

What he had fashioned was not an empire in the commercial sense, but something more lasting: *a kind of civility undergirded by the disciplines of attention, accountability, and patience.*

The roads that led to the crossing grew wider. The parcels near the river changed hands. A warehouse was added, then a depot, and in time, a customs stall and weigh station. Yet each new fixture bore, in its fit and proportion, evidence of the same quiet hand. He had not invented the place, but he had made it intelligible—had given its pieces coherence enough that others could follow without confusion, or fear of overreach.

After his death, the bridge changed hands more than once. Some tried to modernize its span, to widen the planks or streamline the toll procedures. A few spoke of turning it private, of fencing off access after dark. But for all the modifications proposed, little ever truly stuck. Each effort to recast the place seemed to falter against an unspoken contour—a frame of intention laid down long before.

There was something in its construction, in the old ledgers and the regularity of maintenance, that resisted embellishment, not only out of nostalgia, but out of an enduring sense that it had once been done correctly.

It was a legacy, in every sense.

And in the silent aftermath—after the hearing, the verdict, and the weary procession back from the grave—it fell not to committee or corporation, but to the woman who had stood beside him across three decades of relocation, reconciliation, and private industry.

Nellie Loomis Parsons answered inquiries with economy. Gave no discount for sentiment. And in time, those who came to negotiate began to understand that her restraint was not absence, but a kind of rigor. She bore the mantle of oversight with a quiet steadiness, embodying the very virtues her husband had prized—order, fidelity, and resolve.

In an era when widows were often expected to fade into the background, she instead assumed a role both uncommon and essential: guardian of the family's holdings and arbiter of their future.

Through her careful stewardship, Nellie left her children not only the foundations of property and modest incomes but also the tools to build lives of integrity and purpose.

She ensured that each daughter received an education— enough to manage correspondence, understand land divisions, and speak with confidence in legal or civic matters. These capacities, paired with the stamina cultivated under her example, meant they inherited not idle privilege, but quiet competence and moral agency.

They had come, both families, by water and will.

Joseph Loomis arrived in the New World bearing little more than skill and conviction, and he built not only a home but a framework: of land stewardship, communal responsibility, and intellectual striving. Though centuries passed, that foundation held. His descendants, shaped by the hardness of winters and the rigors of self-governance, would chart constellations, establish schools, and weather scandal without turning inward. Through each upheaval, the Loomis name held firm—not for its prominence, but for its constancy.

Jethro Parsons, plowing the northern reaches of Vermont, left behind fewer written records and no illusions. His world was one of frostbitten mornings and wordless tenacity. Yet it was from that plain discipline that something profound was handed forward: an ethic of service, a belief in labor's quiet dignity. It threaded through cavalry boots at Gettysburg, echoed in legal briefs drawn at twilight, and endured through the raw ache of public scandal.

In Nellie and Henry, those two inheritances—conviction and constancy—met not as contradiction, but as complement. Together, they built a household where every gesture carried intention. Their days moved with quiet regularity: morning walks along the property line, ledgers balanced after supper, decisions made shoulder to shoulder with neither dominance nor doubt.

Until Henry's life, and with it their promised future, was extinguished too soon.

And yet, not all was lost.

What had been cultivated between them did not vanish with Henry's passing. It merely transferred, quietly, into the hands of their daughters.

And from those hands, it passed again—sometimes haltingly, sometimes with surer grip—into the grasp of generations, who, though scattered by geography and altered by time, bore within them some quiet echo of the first convictions: the instinct to build with care, to endure without spectacle, to shoulder what must be borne.

What had begun in the furrows of Essex and the wind-brushed banks of the Connecticut did not dissolve into abstraction. It moved—modestly, generationally—into the marrow of a lineage that chose, again and again, to remain anchored to something older than themselves: not legacy for its own sake, but the discipline of having belonged.

Civil War Monument
First Regiment Vermont Cavalry
First Brigade, Third Division Cavalry
Gettysburg, PA

Left - The Jefferson Cottage
Next to Left - Appledoor Cottage
Center - Forest Inn Hotel
Right – Pavillion
Natural Bridge, VA, Campus

Maud Parsons with Lilly (horse) and George (dog)
1872 - 1934

The Jefferson Cottage
Parsons Family Home
Natural Bridge, VA

Col. Henry Chester Parsons
1840 - 1894

John H. Parsons
Died 1863 in Washington DC Hospital

Nelly Jane Loomis Parsons and Gretchen 'Grace' Parsons

Kate, Maud, and Grace Parsons

Maud, Kate, and Grace Parsons

Oil Painting by Nancy Taylor Taliaferro

Daughter of Grace Parsons Brinton

Fan (dog), Kate, friend, Maud, and Grace Parsons Late 1880s –
The Jefferson Cottage

Katherine 'Kate' Parsons

1868 - 1929

Now – Taylor Hall

In 1914, five Loomis siblings pooled their estates to establish a secondary school and in 1914 the Loomis Institute began. It is now a private high school.

The Ship - Susan and Ellen

*Joseph Loomis & family of Braintree, England sailed 1639 and
landed in Boston, MA*

1829-1825 brother of Emily Dickinson, lover of Mable Loomis Todd. William Austin Dickinson.

Emily Dickinson

1830 - 1886

The original building of the Loomis Chaffee School

1640 - Loomis Homestead

1856 - 1932 Mable Loomis Todd Gathered and Published Emily Dickson poems. Lover of Emily Dickinson's brother Austin.

Mabel Loomis Todd portrait and signature

The hotel where Col. Parsons was shot – Later changed to C&O Hospital (1896)

From the Collection of Chesapeake and Ohio Historical Society

Clifton Forge, VA

About the Author

Patricia is a first-time author whose inspiration was instilled in her, by her mother, who throughout her childhood told her intimate stories of her family, handed down through diaries, letters, scrapbooks and word of mouth for over two hundred years.

It was quite literally through those stories that she developed a compelling sense of belonging in the scheme of life. A place we only experience through knowing our ancestry.

Patricia holds a bachelor's and master's degrees from The Pennsylvania State University. She grew up and lives in State College, PA.